BROKEN SOUL

CHIPO MANYEMWE

BROKEN SOUL

atmosphere press

© 2025 Chipo Manyemwe

Published by Atmosphere Press

Cover design by Felipe Betim

No part of this book may be reproduced without permission from the author except in brief quotations and in reviews. This is a work of fiction, and any resemblance to real places, persons, or events is entirely coincidental.

Atmospherepress.com

To **God**
For blessing me with the talent of writing. Thank you, God, for this gift.

To my mom, **Lenny Manyemwe**
You always have supported me and still support me in everything I do. Thank you so much for your love.

To my dad, **Johannes Manyemwe**
You surely fulfilled your promise to help me publish a book. Thank you for making my dream a reality.

To my **little** brother, **Farai Manyemwe**
Your belief in my potential and the encouragement you gave me is something I will forever appreciate.

To my little sister, **Chiedza R Manyemwe**
For literally staying up with me till 2am just listening to me tell you the plots of my stories. I truly treasure you.

To my friend group:

Anotidaishe G Chirenje
My BFFAE [Best Friend Forever And Ever], thank you for your love, support, insight and just your presence in my life, which has been of great impact.

Tanaka C Machawira
The mother of the group. You basically foreshadowed my future by nicknaming me "Miss Author" for years till it became a reality.

Tinomudaishe R C Madhara
The cool kid of the group. Thank you for the moral support and confidence in me.

To my closest friends:

Siobhan R Hombarume
Thank you for lending me your ears whenever I felt like storytelling, for comforting me and always believing in me.

Tafadzwa C Mwanunura
Thank you for always checking up on me, especially when it came to my mental health, as well as always believing I would make it.

Shelly R Marias
The most avid bookworm I know. Thank you for making me love to write.

Musawenkosi Mpofu
Thank you for always finding a way to make me smile, and for your unwavering belief in me.

TABLE OF CONTENTS

Prologue 1

Chapter 1 3
Chapter 2 24
Chapter 3 38
Chapter 4 71
Chapter 5 80
Chapter 6 88
Chapter 7 99
Chapter 8 104

Epilogue 106

References 109

Trigger Warning: This book contains suicide, eating disorders, attempted rape and self-harm.

PROLOGUE

Approximately 20% of teens nowadays go through depression before adulthood. Depression can be defined as a mental health disorder that is associated with the lowering of a person's mood. Teenagers have different reasons for being depressed, and this can lead to getting into antisocial behaviors like drug abuse and some to the extent of suicide. Depression can be associated with anxiety disorders and can get as serious as being bipolar. Anxiety is intense, excessive and persistent worry and fear about everyday situations. Bipolar is a disorder associated with episodes of mood swings ranging from depressive lows to manic highs. The exact cause of bipolar disorder isn't known, but a combination of genetics, environment, altered brain structure and chemistry may play a role. Manic episodes may include symptoms such as high energy, reduced need for sleep and loss of touch with reality. Depressive episodes may include symptoms such as low energy, low motivation and loss of interest in daily activities. Mood episodes last days to months at a time and may also be associated with suicidal thoughts.

Approximately 19.2% of students aged 12-18, enrolled in grades 6-12, experienced bullying nationwide during the 2021-2022 school year. Among students aged 12-18 in grades 6-12 who reported being bullied, roughly 2 in 3 reported being bullied on multiple days during the school year. Bullying is when one is made fun of, picked on, made to feel bad, emotionally abused or physically abused by a person who thinks they are bigger or more powerful than the person being bullied. Cyberbullying is the use of technology to harass, threaten, embarrass, or target another person through threats and mean, aggressive, or rude texts, tweets, posts, or messages. About 37% of young people between the ages of 12 and 17 have been bullied online, and 30% have had it happen more than once.

Body Dysmorphia can also be known as Body Dysmorphic Disorder [BDD]. It is a mental illness characterized by constant worrying over a *perceived or slight defect in appearance. According to a survey by Mental Health Foundation, they found out that 35% of teenagers worry about their body image often or every day, and 37% of teenagers feel upset and ashamed about their body image. The cause of BDD is thought to be a combination of environmental, psychological, and biological factors. Bullying or teasing may create feelings of inadequacy, shame, and fear of ridicule. Having a negative image of one's body can lead to a higher risk of depression or an eating disorder.*

With the above research from the prologue, this book brings to life this information. I hope and would like readers to make that connection. So, with that, enough of the educational talk, let's talk about a young girl by the name Samantha Carter who was a 16-year-old girl. She lived in the humble town of Middletown. She lived with two parents and an older brother. Her father, Mr Kevin Carter, was a professor at the University of Middletown, while her mother, Sabrina Carter, was a secretary at a local business firm. Her brother, Liam Carter, was two years older than she was and also went to the same high school she went to, which was known as Cougar High. It had been a sunshine Christmas, but it was all over, and now it was back to hardcore school work.

CHAPTER 1

Sabrina: Kids, we are going to be late on the first day!
Liam: (Coming downstairs) We're coming.
Sabrina: Samantha!
Samantha: (Coming downstairs) Sorry Mom, I couldn't zip my dress.
Liam: (Sarcastically) I wonder why?
Sabrina: (Nudging Liam) Stop it. (To Samantha) Come here, Sammy. I'll zip you up.
Samantha: (With a sigh) Thank you.
Sabrina: There you go.
Kevin: You people are still here? (Giving Sabrina a kiss)
Sabrina: Yea, we're late.
Samantha: Man, this dress is too small.
Kevin: (Taking an apple) Or you are just too big.
Sabrina: Honey!
Kevin: What? It's the truth this Christmas she gained a couple kilograms. It's a fact. Well I'm off.
Sabrina: Ignore him, Sam. We'll get you new dresses.
Samantha: (With a sigh) It's alright.
Sabrina: Let's go, and don't forget your lunches.

In the car.

Sabrina: So, do you two have plans for this amazing summer term?
Liam: I'm joining the football team.

Samantha: I'm joining the cheer squad.
Liam: (Laughing) Yeah, right.
Samantha: What Liam?
Liam: Do you know Kenzie?
Samantha: What about her?
Liam: She's all about looks, and no offense, but your look isn't the look.
Samantha: What is that supposed to mean?
Liam: Well... you are....
Sabrina: Cut it out Liam.
Liam: Mom I'm just saying it so as to protect her and avoid her getting humiliated.
Sabrina: Well, even if she's fat...

Liam burst out a laugh.

Sabrina: ...I mean stout. That has nothing to do with her not being given a chance to participate in the cheer team.

Samantha just sighed and looked out the window.

Liam: We'll see about that.

They got to the school and they both came out of the car.

Sabrina: Bye kids.
Liam and Samantha: (In chorus) Bye Mom.
Liam: Listen, no offense Sam, but I don't want to be seen around you. It would ruin my chances this summer.
Samantha: What are you talking about?
Liam: Look at you. I mean, it's embarrassing to walk around with a sumo fighter of a sister.
Samantha: What?
Liam: Just please pretend like you don't know me.
Samantha: Owwkay.

Weighing 60 kg [132 lbs.] was just enough to be basically disowned by her brother. Liam went into the school first, while Samantha followed way behind. People just stared and looked at her as if she was disgusting. She felt so weird.

Tony: Hey Sammy.
Samantha: Hey Tony (closing her locker)
Tony: How was your...
Samantha: What is it?
Tony: Uh, nothing.
Samantha: Let me guess. It's my weight, isn't it?
Tony: What? Nooo way. I actually hadn't noticed.
Samantha: You are just saying that. I know. I just gained a little weight.
Tony: You do know it's not always about looks. Right Sam?
Samantha: Yea you're right. Oh my gosh, is that Randy?
Tony: (With a sigh) Yea, he got ripped this Christmas holiday.
Samantha: (Dreamily) I see that. I hope he asks me to the dance this year.
Tony: (Staring at a Samantha who wasn't even looking at him) You want to go with him?
Samantha: Well, of course. He is my major crush. He's so dreamy.
Tony: (Looking aside) If you say so Samantha.

They went to class. People were chitchatting with one another as they waited for their teacher. Samantha was just finishing up some notes when Katey walked up to her.

Katey: Samantha, heyyy.
Samantha: (Nervously) Hi Katey.
Katey: You know I didn't even notice you. I mean, can you blame me?
Samantha: I'm sorry...I don't think I understand.
Katey: (Whispering in her ear) You got fat.
Samantha: Um, no, it's just that I gained a little.
Katey: Yea, right. You have to find a way to lose it. Otherwise,

you never know where you'll end up.
Miss Paris: How is everyone?
Everyone: We are fine and you!?
Katey: Just some advice to digest (walking away to her seat).

Samantha just tried to brush it off, that is until she raised her hand to answer a question.

Miss Paris: Um, who can answer this? Um, are you new here dear?

Samantha just pointed at herself.

Miss Paris: Yes.
Samantha: Uh, no, it's Samantha.
Miss Paris: Oh my. You, um, look...different.
Katey: Right!

Everyone except Tony started laughing.

Miss Paris: Okay, that's enough! Yes, Samantha.
Samantha: (Looking down) They are drip tip leaves.
Miss Paris: Exactly.

Samantha felt so embarrassed, but that was just the trigger to the gunshot. There was more to come.

They had a science lesson.

Mr Gregory: So fatty foods are unhealthy.

Everyone stared at Samantha and she just looked down.

Mr Gregory: Can anyone tell me what problems can arise from eating them?

Troy: Heart diseases.
Mr Gregory: Yes Troy. Anything else.
Mia: High blood pressure.
Mr Gregory: Yes Mia. More answers.
Ben: Diabetes.

Mr Gregory: Correct Ben. I'm still looking for the most obvious answer. Anybody?

Samantha slowly raised her hand.

Mr Gregory: Yes, um...

Samantha: Obesity.
Mr Gregory: Yes, uh...
Katey: Obese Samantha!
Mr Gregory: Woah Samantha, is that you?
Samantha: Yes sir.
Mr Gregory: You really have changed.
Katey: Full of fatty flesh. Maybe she could present on obesity so we understand better (laughing).

Everyone except Tony burst into laughter.

Mr Gregory: Alright everyone, pipe down. There is no need to say that. Right Katey?
Katey: (Rolling her eyes) Yes, Mr Gregory.
Mr Gregory: Okay, here is some homework.

After a few days, Katey came up to Samantha during lunch.

Katey: Look, Sammy, look.
Samantha: What?
Katey: Check this out (blowing a bubble-gum, then it pops).
Samantha: So?

Katey: Now we know what's going to happen to you next (walking away in sly laughter).
Tony: Are you alright?
Samantha: I guess.
Tony: I'm really sorry about what has happened lately to you.
Samantha: It's fine.
Tony: So, what are you trying out this year?
Samantha: I was thinking of cheerleading.
Tony: Oh, okay. That would be great. You used to always want to join it.
Samantha: I'm going to go for tryouts on Friday.
Tony: You'll be great.

Samantha went with her mom to get new dresses for school.

Store assistant: This dress is also too small.
Sabrina: Then get the biggest size!
Store assistant: This is the biggest size.
Sabrina: Are you kidding me?
Store assistant: No.
Sabrina: Urgh, why did you have to get so fat, Samantha?
Store assistant: It's not a problem, ma'am. You could personalize her dresses.
Sabrina: Oh, then we'll do that.
Store assistant: Though there is an extra fee because of taking her measurements and sewing from the start.
Sabrina: Great. See Samantha what your fattiness is causing for us?
Store assistant: Ma'am, she's not fat. She's just a little stout.
Sabrina: Don't tell me how to speak to my child. Argh, here's your the money.

Samantha's measurements were taken and her new dresses were made.

On Friday, Samantha went for tryouts.

Kenzie: You are definitely going to be part of the cheer squad Theresa.
Theresa: Thank you, Kenzie (shaking her pompoms).
Kenzie: Now... Next!!!
Felicia: Kenzie, do you really have to yell?
Kenzie: How else would those povos hear me?
Tracy: (In a perky tone) Kenzie is right. We don't have all day.
Samantha: (Walking in).
Kenzie: Woah, woah. Stop right there.
Samantha: Is there a problem?
Kenzie: Uhhhh. Isn't it obvious?
Samantha: No.
Felicia: Next please.
Tracy: (In a perky tone) Baby, you're a fatty.
Kenzie: Now, now you two. Play nice. I mean, be the **bigger** people.

Tracy and Felicia started laughing.

Tracy: (Laughing) I see what you did there.
Felicia: (Laughing) Nice one.
Kenzie: Thank you. Now Sally.
Samantha: That's Sammy.
Kenzie: (Checking her check board) Yeah, yeah, whatever. For someone to be part of my cheer squad, you have to have...
Felicia: A fever for cheer.
Tracy: The flair and glare.
Kenzie: The cheer posture and my personal favorite (getting closer to her). My liking towards you. So, with that...
Kenzie, Felicia and Tracy: (In chorus) NEXT!!!
Kenzie: Now scram, you overfed pig.
Patricia: S.U....

Kenzie: Patricia!
Patricia: Uh, yeah.
Kenzie: Well, it's obvious that you are part of the cheer squad. You were always the best gymnast in our class ever since grade 3.
Patricia: Well...that's not really accurate. It was Samantha. I was second best.
Kenzie: Well, to me it seemed and seems you deserved it more (looking at Samantha).
Tracy: (Jumping up and down) Welcome to the squad.
Felicia: Here are your pompoms.
Patricia: Wow. Thank you, guys.

Samantha walked out of the courts like a wet puppy in the rain. Streams formed on her caramel-brown cheeks.

Tony: Hey, Sam. How were tryouts?
Samantha: (Closing her locker) What do you think?
Tony: Yiiish! Why are your eyes so bloodshot?
Samantha: Because Tony, that brat Kenzie refused that I join her cheer squad. She called me an overfed pig. An overfed pig!
Tony: Hey, don't let her get to you. Maybe cheerleading just isn't...
Samantha: Isn't my thing! Isn't my thing, Tony! Nonsense. I'm a cheerleader. I know it.
Tony: Yes, ma'am. So, what now?
Samantha: I'm going to find a way to get into that cheer squad even if it's the last thing I do.
Tony: That's the Samantha I know.

Tony and Samantha went to his house. There she met Tony's mom, Tamika. Tony and Samantha had been friends for such a long time that Tony's mom was like a second mom to her.

Tamika: Tony, Samantha!

Samantha and Tony: (In chorus) Hey, Mom.

Tamika: Well, you just came on time because I was just making my famous roast chicken. I know how much you love it Sammy.

Samantha: (With a sigh) Please don't put too much for me.

Tamika: Um, okay (looking at Tony).

While they were eating

Tamika: So, how's school you two?

Tony: It's alright.

Tamika: Samantha?

Samantha: It's the worst.

Tamika: Why is that?

Samantha: People are making fun of the way I look. They call me fat, an overfed pig, a sumo fighter and all those things. I couldn't even get in the cheer squad because of it.

Tamika: Well, I'm fat too, you know, but I don't let anyone else define who I am. I am my own person. If I feel beautiful, then I am beautiful. That's what I always say.

Samantha: You're not even that big, and anyway I have to fit into the societal expectations; otherwise, I don't achieve anything.

Tamika: Samantha, those are unrealistic expectations of women's bodies. We are all built differently and beautifully for that matter.

Samantha: I wish I could believe that.

Tamika: (With a sigh) Samantha, it's your choice, but you have to make sure you are not just living for other people; otherwise, you'll never succeed. If you feel having a smaller body with wide hips, a large bosom and a big posterior will make you feel good about yourself, then fine, but everything has its own problems, and there are risks and consequences for everything we do.

At first, Samantha took the words she heard from Tony's mom to heart, but when she got home and looked at herself in the mirror, those words became non-existent. She went back to feeling anxious about how she looked and decided to search on the internet for ways to reduce her weight. That's when she came across a site that almost caused her to lose her life. After every meal she ate, she would put her fingers in her mouth and force herself to vomit. She kept doing it, and then one day at school...

Tony: Hey Sam, are you okay? You don't look so good.
Samantha: I'm fine, don't worry about me.

During the Geo lesson.

Samantha: Miss Paris, may I please be excused?
Miss Paris: Uh yes, um...
Samantha: Samantha.
Miss Paris: Are you okay, dear?
Samantha: Yes.
Miss Paris: You can go.

Samantha went to the ablutions, and she vomited like never before. She then came out and was making her way to the classroom when...

Tony: Sam, you don't look good. What's up?
Samantha: I'm...I'm...

Samantha then collapsed. Luckily, Miss Paris had decided to follow Sam and see if she was okay.

Miss Paris: Oh no. Tony, go call the principal and tell her it's an emergency!

Tony: Yes, ma'am.

The principal called an ambulance, which arrived and took Samantha to the hospital. At the hospital, the doctor found out what Samantha had been doing and told her parents that she had been diagnosed with Bulimia. She had been doing it for a while now, and her body couldn't take it anymore, so it shut down. He advised them to watch her carefully and ensure she didn't do it again. She was then let out of the hospital.

In the car.

Kevin: Are you proud of yourself, Samantha? Hey, young lady, I'm talking to you!
Sabrina: Samantha Hope Carter! Your father is talking to you!
Samantha: (In a whisper) No.
Kevin: What did you think you were going to achieve by doing such a thing?
Liam: Weight loss?
Sabrina: Well, instead, she almost achieved death. Death Samantha! Death!
Samantha: (In a whisper) I'm sorry.
Kevin: You better be.

This would have been the perfect time to cue the song by Maddie Zahm, *Fat Funny Friend*.
Tony was told what had been happening and decided to pay his best friend a visit.

Tony: Afternoon Mrs Carter.
Sabrina: Afternoon dear. She's up in her room.
Tony: Thank you.
Sabrina: You teenagers nowadays make no sense. Bulimia, what is that?
Tony: I got you flowers.

Sabrina: Oh, thank you. You are such a darling.
Tony: Anytime.

Tony went upstairs to Samantha's room.

Tony: (Knocking on the door) Hey, it's Tony.
Samantha: (Opening the door) Come in.
There was a silence for a while until Tony broke it with a question that he already knew the answer to.

Tony: But why Sammy? Why?
Samantha: Look at me. I'm just a ball of fatty flesh. I wanted to get rid of it.
Tony: So, bulimia was the solution?
Samantha: I didn't have any other.
Tony: You could have died.
Samantha: But I didn't.
Tony: (With a scoff) I can't believe you. Here are your flowers.
Samantha: Thank you.
Tony: You don't need to lose weight. You are amazing the way you are.
Samantha: You are only going to say that since I'm your friend, otherwise everyone else doesn't. It's either I shape in or I shape out. That's just the world we live in.
Tony: No Samantha, it's the world you want to live in, where you want to feed unrealistic expectations of a woman, of a girl. It's not what's on the outside that matters but what's on the inside. If you keep doing this, you are going to end nowhere. Mark my words. Bye Samantha.
Samantha: Bye Tony.

Samantha felt like no one could understand her and it made her hurt so bad. She was shouting so loud, but no one could hear her. Trying to maintain her balance on an acrobatic strip but falling into a bottomless pit. Grabbing hold of an edge but losing her grip and losing herself. That's what Samantha felt.

There was even a time she was supposed to present at assembly.

Principal Penolopy: For the weather report, Samantha Carter.
Everyone applauded.

As she made her way to the stage, she could feel her voice slipping away and the weakness in her knees. She started hearing all that delusional laughter of people laughing at her and mocking her for the way she looked. She just couldn't do it.

Samantha: (Looking down) Sorry, Principal Penolopy.
Principal Penolopy: Uh, um...
Everyone: Huh?

Samantha just left the stage and the hall.

Principal: Well, the weather for today is going to be...

After assembly in class.

Katey: Wow. So not only is she a puffed-up balloon, but she's a scaredy-cat (with a scoff). Pathetic.
Tony: Ignore her, Sam.

Samantha nodded her head with a sigh.

She posted a picture of herself on Instagram hoping to get some love from people, but that was the exact opposite of what she ended up getting.

These were some of the comments in the comment section:

"When I first saw it, I thought someone was using a filter to enhance their size to then see that it's her actual size."
"Are you sure when you step on a scale it doesn't say to be continued..."

"Are you preg?"
"That's one well-fed fat cow... Oh wait, it's a human being."
"You look old when you are that fat."
"You're only 16, but look like you're in your mid-20s."
"Someone's got a mid-wife wine body."
"I'm a doctor and I'm concerned about your eating habits. Being fat can lead to a lot of health problems, so eat greens; otherwise, your lifeline is fading and fading quickly."
"If she faints, I bet people just roll her."

You would wonder when someone was writing that, were they conscious or do they even have a conscience? If you have nothing good to say, then don't say anything at all because saying something bad doesn't make you cool. It makes you mean and cruel. Samantha, after reading this and so many more, deleted the post. It was just too much.

There is also a time they went to church.

Sabrina: Everybody, let's move, we don't want to be late.
Samantha: I'm done.
Sabrina: My, my, your body is so out of shape. I hadn't realized how fat you were. You have to do something. I mean, look, you are basically suffocating that dress. Don't you have anything bigger to wear?
Samantha: (Looking down) No. I could stay at home if you want.
Sabrina: Ridiculous, let's go. Can you also fit through the door?
Samantha: (Rolling her eyes) Yes.

At the church.

Sabrina: Oh, dang it, there's Mary. I can't afford to let her see you.
Samantha: Why?
Sabrina: Isn't it obvious? (Shaping her body in a round form).

Mary: Sabrina!
Sabrina: Maryyy! What a pleasure to see you.
Mary: Well, it's good to be back home with Craig. He was getting a little homesick.
Sabrina: Naww, how was Florida?
Mary: Marvelous darling, and how is my daughter-in... Woah.
Sabrina: I know.
Mary: At first, I thought she got pregnant. She got fat.
Sabrina: Yes.
Mary: (Whispering to Sabrina) You better start reducing someone's portions of food.
Sabrina: (Whispering back) I know, I'll do that.
Samantha: Still standing right here ladies.
Craig: Mom, how long are we... Samantha!
Samantha: Hi Craig.
Craig: What happened to you? You look like some hippo.
Mary: (Slightly laughing) Now, Craig.
Craig: I'm just saying.
Mary: I'll see you around Sabrina, and don't forget... (in a whisper and pointing at Samantha) portions.
Sabrina: Yeah. Oh my gosh, that was humiliating.
Samantha: It was.
Sabrina: (Mockingly) It was. Well, maybe if you didn't look so fat, this wouldn't be a problem. It's such an utter disgrace being with you.
Samantha: (In a whisper) I did suggest to stay at home.

A few weeks passed and they took tests on all the subjects they did.

Mr Richards: The highest in literature is obviously...
Everyone: Samantha!
Mr Richards: ...scoring full marks, Samantha Carter. Wait a minute. Who is this?
Samantha: It's Samantha.
Mr Richards: What happened to you?

Katey: She got fat!

Everyone except Tony laughed.

Tony: Sir, don't you think it's not right for people to laugh at her?
Mr Richards: No Tony, they should laugh because look at her. I mean, you look so out of shape. Do you even have one? You look like some GMO tomato.

Everyone laughed harder.

Mr Richards: And what do you want to be in the future?
Samantha: (In a whisper) A psychologist.
Mr Richards: (Laughing) And you think looking like that you will become a psychologist. All the psychologists I know have gorgeous bodies and definitely not bodies like yours. I mean, they are slim and slender and have the right **fat** in the right places. You know what, you don't deserve these marks. I'm giving you a 95%.
Samantha: But sir, that's not fair. I didn't get anything wrong.
Mr Richards: But your body is wrong. You don't expect me to say I'm raising a psychologist and you look like that. I'll be a laughing stock.
Samantha: This is just about my appear...
Mr Richards: Just shut it and accept that your body is disgusting. Disgusting to look at and disgusting to be in.
Everyone: Oooo Oooo!!!
Mr Richards: Here's your exam paper. Go sit down!
Samantha: (Reaching to get her paper and tearing the seam under the armpit of her dress) Oops.
Mr Richards: (Sarcastically) Shocker. Hopefully, you also won't break the chair.

Everyone laughed once again. The bell then rang.

Mr Richards: Okay everyone, come and get your papers.

Samantha left the classroom first with red jalapeno eyes and sniffling all the way to the lunchroom. She sat at a table by herself like a loner. She felt empty and numb. How could he say that to her? How could he humiliate her like that? Was her body really disgusting? She was interrupted in the middle of her thoughts by somebody she did not even expect.

Randy: Heyy. Samantha, right?
Samantha: Yes.
Randy: Wow, I didn't even notice you there. I mean, is it like you were on a 600-pound diet or something?

Randy's teammates just laughed.

Randy: I'm just saying (sitting down next to her). To get to the extent of the fattiness you got, you must have been on that diet.
Samantha: Please just leave me alone Randy.
Randy: I'm just saying it how I see it (sarcastically). Oh, I get it, you were on a cow or pig's diet. Well, it took a toll on you Samantha.
Samantha: Just...
Tony: Leave her alone Randy!
Randy: (Sarcastically) Oh well, your boyfriend is here. Unfortunately, I'm a vegetarian, so I don't want any beef Tony (snickering). I will be taking that too (taking Samantha's chicken and eating it). You'll pop soon if you keep eating like this.

Randy went to where his teammates were and started getting hyped up by them as if what he had done was honorable.

Tony: Ey Sam, don't listen to him. Appearances don't mean...
Samantha: (Wiping her tears) Just don't Tony. You don't understand because you aren't fat. I'm just tired of it. This entire term has all been about how I have ballooned. I've made up mind Tony. I'm going to lose all this excess fat this holiday. That's final.
Tony: Are you sure about that?
Samantha: (Taking a big sigh and wiping her final tears) Yes.

When she got home, her brother gave his report card to their parents first.

Liam: Check it out.
Sabrina: Oh, wow, 6As and 4Bs!
Kevin: That's impressive, Liam! I'm proud of you.
Sabrina: Samantha, what of you? Bring your report card.
Samantha: I tried (giving her report card to her mom).
Sabrina: 6As, 2Bs and 2Cs.
Kevin: Where are these 2Cs coming from?
Sabrina: Accounts and Math.
Kevin: What!? The professor's child failing such subjects. Impossible! Give me that (snatching the report from Sabrina). Samantha, what is this?
Samantha: I said I tried.
Kevin: Getting A's in useless subjects such as History, Geo and Literature. LITERATURE Samantha!
Samantha: I actually don't need Math and Accounts for what I want to become. I actually need Literature.
Kevin: There is nowhere you can go without Math, so don't tell me such nonsense.
Sabrina: You will have to work harder, Samantha. Be more like your brother.
Kevin: I agree with your mother. Otherwise, you won't amount to anything in life. Here's your report card (throwing it to her).
Samantha: (In a whisper) So the 6As mean nothing?

Kevin: What was that, Samantha!?
Samantha: Nothing.
Kevin: That's what I thought.
Samantha: Actually, I was kindly asking if you could speak to the principal to take me out of Mr Richards' class and maybe into Mrs Hudgens' instead.
Kevin: And why would I do that?
Samantha: Well, the teacher is verbally abusing me.
Sabrina: What did he say to you?
Samantha: He called me disgusting and a GMO tomato.
Liam: (Laughing) GMO tomato. Sis!
Sabrina: Well, maybe if you didn't have such a body then you wouldn't have to deal with that.
Kevin: I agree with your mom. So, you're not getting out of that class.
Sabrina: It's two terms with him left anyway.
Samantha: (With a sigh) If you say so.

Samantha: I can't believe you.
Liam: What?
Samantha: You knew very well that I wanted to show them my report first, and you gave yours first.
Liam: Well, it's already been done, so...
Samantha: You are unbelievable.
Liam: And you are fat.
Samantha: That has nothing to do with anything we are talking about and you know it.
Liam: Whatever fatty, or should I say GMO tomato? (Laughing) Why aren't you laughing with me?
Samantha: Because it's not funny. Just leave me alone.

Samantha made her way to her room and cried bitterly. It broke her that her brother was such a jerk and her parents were so difficult. They did not even seem to care about her. Loneliness consumed her and it was scary and heart-breaking. If only they could understand what she was going through. In the evening, she decided to write in her trusty diary.

06/04/21

Dear Diary

This term has been such a wreck. I have been called names and made fun of. Being 16 is not at all what I dreamed it would be. I've been called fat, obese, a GMO tomato, out of shape, a hippo, a sumo fighter and most painful of all, disgusting. There is even a girl who blew a bubble-gum and let it pop and told me that's where I'm heading. My major crush also asked if I was taking a 600-pound diet. Argh, it was so embarrassing. I couldn't even get into the cheer squad because of how I look. My literature teacher humiliated me in class. My mom says I'm a disgrace to walk with, and my father is always attacking me for the way I look. Mr Richards called me disgusting. I can't take this anymore. I've been asking myself and looking at myself in the mirror, and I think they are right. I need to change the way I look, my appearance and fit into the societal expectations, otherwise I will never get anything. So goodbye old self and new self, can't wait to meet you.

Samantha Hope Carter

After writing this in her diary, she decided to start working on herself.

The first thing she did was get in contact with someone who could provide her with something she needed but could not get legally. Samantha made a phone call to meet up with one of her friends, Tendai, who she met up with at the back of Tendai's grandmother's grocery store. Tendai was known for selling illegal things and that is exactly what Samantha wanted.

Samantha: Hey. You have the stuff?
Tendai: Sammy. Hey. Yeah, I got Liraglutide (Saxenda) injections.
Samantha: Injections? Tendai, you know how much I fear needles.
Tendai: Okay, great then. You don't need them; I'll just be on my way and will see you in school.

Samantha: (Grabbing Tendai) Tendai please. I need this.
Tendai: Trust me, you don't. I feel so guilty right now giving you these. If it was someone I don't know, well, I wouldn't feel as bad.
Samantha: This is for my health though.
Tendai: It definitely isn't, it's unprescribed.
Samantha: I just want to feel good in my skin Tendai. Please.
Tendai: (With a sigh) Fine. (Handing Samantha the injections) So it's a 30-day course thing, and since we are left with 29 days till the end of the holiday, you are still on schedule. The first week you will take 0.6mg, the second week you will take 1.2mg, the third week you will take 1.8mg, the fourth week 2.4mg, and the fifth week, 3mg.
Samantha: Okay, got it. Here is your money.
Tendai: Thank you.
Samantha: No, thank you.
Tendai: Please stay safe Samantha, okay?
Samantha: (With a slight smile) I will.

The entire holiday she worked on losing weight. She reduced her food portions and exercised more while working with a strict slimming diet, which made her lose 4kg (9 lbs.). The Liraglutide (Saxenda) injections made her lose 3kg (7 lbs.). She would wake up in the morning, run around the neighborhood and sometimes go to the gym. Although she had been warned not to do it, out of pure desperation, Samantha still practiced bulimia, which made her lose 3kg (7 lbs.).

The holiday came to an end after 5 splendid weeks; it was now May, and it was time for the winter term to begin.

CHAPTER 2

Sabrina: Guys, let's go!
Liam: I'm already done.
Sabrina: Samantha, let's get going!
Samantha: May you please zip me up.
Liam: Yikes!
Samantha: What?
Sabrina: You lost a lot of weight.
Samantha: (Smiling) You noticed.
Liam: Well, now you look like a...
Sabrina: We don't have time. Let's get going (zipping Samantha). This means new dresses.
Kevin: Bye honey. What on Earth! Samantha!
Samantha: Yes Dad. Is there a problem?
Kevin: Well, if you mean looking like you could be blown away by a gale of wind, then yeah, there is a problem. You make it seem like we weren't feeding you.
Liam: (Laughing) More like a gust of wind.
Sabrina: What should be more worrying is buying new dresses.
Samantha: But I thought losing weight would solve the problem. It's all you guys would talk about and make fun of me at the same time.
Kevin: Well now we have something else to make fun of. You look skinny.
Sabrina: We can talk about this later on. Let's get going.

Samantha just grabbed her lunch and left first for the car. She was puzzled. They had been complaining about how fat she was, and now they were complaining that she was skinny. It didn't make any sense to her.

Liam: So is this your idea of the right look?
Samantha: I lost weight, didn't I?
Liam: Yea, and yet it still isn't the look.
Samantha: Leave me alone Liam.
Sabrina: Are you still trying out for cheerleading?
Samantha: Yes.
Sabrina: Are you sure you can lift the pompoms?
Samantha: MOM!
Liam: (Laughing) Good question.
Sabrina: Doesn't matter. Good riddance to that fat self of yours, but we have to get new uniforms.
Samantha: (Mumbling) Of course.

Their mom dropped them off at school.

Liam: So, you know the drill.
Samantha: What drill?
Liam: Pretend like you don't know me.
Samantha: But I'm no longer fat.
Liam: But you are skinny, and I can't walk around with a stickman for a sister. So...
Samantha: Are you kidding me!? You know what, just go.

Now she weighed 50kg [110 lbs.] but still was being disowned by her brother. She followed after him, and people just glared at her as if she was some creature from another planet.

Tony: Sa...
Samantha: What Tony?
Tony: You lost weight.

Samantha: Yeah. Is it bad?
Tony: Uh, no, why would you think that?
Samantha: People are just staring at me weirdly.
Tony: Maybe it's just because you lost that so-called excess fat.
Samantha: (With a sigh) Maybe.
Katey: What in the...
Samantha: What is it Katey?
Katey: You.
Samantha: What about me?
Katey: You look like a human stick insect.
Samantha: What!?
Katey: I'm just...
Tony: Just leave her alone Katey.

Samantha just stormed away and went to class. She had lessons and teacher after teacher did not even recognize her.

Miss Paris: Anyone to give me the answer? Mmmm Samantha, is that you?
Samantha: Yes.
Miss Paris: Are you feeling well or were you sick during the holiday?
Samantha: Uh, no. Why do you ask?
Miss Paris: I mean, you lost so much weight.

Everyone except Tony just laughed.

Miss Paris: Silence everyone!
Samantha: I lost it myself.
Miss Paris: Well... o...kay. Anyway, what's the answer?
Samantha: It's a herbivore.
Miss Paris: Yes.

She then went with her mom to get new dresses.

Shop assistant: Ma'am, this dress is the smallest, but it's still really big.
Sabrina: Great! Not again! Do you see Samantha? Your skinniness is causing costs for us.
Shop assistant: We could just...
Sabrina: (Mockingly) ...get personalized dresses. Is that it? This is unbelievable!

Samantha just looked down and, after her measurements were done, they went home. It broke her to think all her hard work had been for nothing. She had a bad feeling that this term was going to feel unbearably long. She went for cheerleading tryouts the following week when they had them.

Felicia: I really don't know why we have to do this every term.
Tracy: (Perky) It's to get the best silly.
Kenzie: Plus, it's just for this year only. Then next year a new cheer team is chosen. Next!

Samantha walked in.

Kenzie: (Laughing) You must be kidding.
Felicia: Is that really you Samantha?
Samantha: Yes.
Tracy: Yikes. Someone wasn't eating this holiday.
Kenzie: Sarah...
Samantha: Samantha.
Kenzie: (Checking her check board) Whatever. Do you think I'm going to risk a paper-thin failing to carry herself and being easily toppled over? Well the answer is a big fat NO!
Samantha: But I lost weight.
Kenzie: Did I say do that? I don't think so. So why don't you take your skinny and unhealthy form of a body out of my tryout space.

Kenzie, Felicia and Tracy: (In chorus) NEXT!!!

Samantha left feeling so disheartened. When she thought she had solved her problem she had actually brought upon herself another problem. She went to the bathroom and cried in heart-breaking bitterness.

Tony: So, Sam, how were...
Samantha: ...Please don't ask.
Tony: Woah. Sammy, your eyes are rash red. What happened?
Samantha: They basically just skinny-shamed me. Kenzie even called me unhealthy.
Tony: Man, that girl is such a spoiled brat.
Samantha: (Drying the tears that were already streaming down her cheeks) Tell me about it.
Tony: Just leave her be. Are you still up for going to my house? My mom is making her famous roast chicken.
Samantha: (Laughing) You always know how to make me smile. Let's get going.

Samantha and Tony went to Tony's house. A place to Samantha that was not just a house but felt more like a home.

Tamika: How are my two favorite...?
Samantha: It's my weight, isn't it?
Tamika: Well...You look good, darling.
Samantha: But I don't feel good.
Tamika: (Putting the food on the table) Why don't we talk about it while we eat my famous roast chicken?

Tony: Absolutely. I'm starved.

Tamika: So, what seems to be the problem?
Samantha: I thought losing weight would solve everything, but it just ruined everything.

Tamika: Well, everything has its risks. Right?

Samantha: Hmm. I know what I did wrong, I just lost too much weight. I'll just fix it.
Tamika: When will you learn that, I repeat, everything has consequences and risks?
Samantha: Don't worry. I know what to do.
Tony: Here we go again.

There was another time again when she was supposed to present at assembly.

Principal Penolopy: For the weather report, Samantha Carter.

Everyone applauded.

Once again, as she made her way to the stage, she could feel her voice slipping away and the weakness in her knees. She started hearing all that delusional laughter of people laughing at her and mocking her for losing weight and becoming slim. Once again, she just couldn't do it.

Samantha: (Looking down) I can't Principal Penolopy.
Principal Penolopy: Uh, again, um...
Everyone: Huh?

Samantha just left the stage and the hall.

Principal Penolopy: Well, the weather for today is going to be...

After assembly in class.

Katey: Wow. Twice in a row the bony princess couldn't present. You are hopeless.
Tony: Ignore her Sam.

Samantha nodded her head with a sigh. After a few days, the

following happened at lunch.
Lunch lady: Samantha, is that you!?
Samantha: Um, yes.
Lunch lady: What happened to you!?
Samantha: What do you mean?
Lunch lady: You look like one of the threads I use to sew!

Everyone just laughed.

Lunch lady: Come here, let me add more food for you.
Samantha: That's really not necessary.
Lunch lady: No, no, give me that (snatching her plate and adding mountains of food).
Samantha: Uh...
Lunch lady: Good girl. Here you go.
Samantha: Um, thanks...

Katey: Sammy, check this out.
Samantha: What is it Katey?
Katey: (Taking out a toothpick and snapping it in half) See.
Samantha: I don't understand.
Katey: That's the future for you if you keep up like this.
Samantha: What do you get from bullying me Katey?
Katey: (Coyishly smiling) Pleasure.

Katey just left her after that bitter word.

Tony: Hey are you okay?
Samantha: I'm fine (standing up and leaving).

Tony just sat there worried about his best friend, slash crush. After what had happened, he wasn't sure what extreme measures she would take.

One day she posted a picture of herself in a yellow body-hugging dress. Her birthday was coming up on the 15th of July.

She also captioned her photo @bdae loading, and she got comments that shattered her.

These were some of the comments:

"Wow, look, it's Mrs bones."
"Literally nobody: @4Sam: Look guys, a picture of me deflated."
"Are you sure you won't be carried away by one of your birthday balloons?"
"I feel sorry for that dress. Being worn by a shapeless creature."
"If you squint a little, tilt your head, flip your phone upside down, it almost looks like there is actually a person."
"Why does she look like a reed?"
"Ey, I don't think there are scales with negative figures, because with that body you're striking a negative number for sure.

There were lots more. She decided to delete the picture and not have a birthday party at all. People were cruel and were such unnecessary critics.

A few weeks passed and it was a windy day.

Sabrina: Bye kids!
Liam and Samantha: (In chorus) Bye!!

Randy: Check it out guys. Skinny Sam is not flying away like a kite.

His teammates laughed.

Todd: Maybe she has stones in her backpack to hold her down.

Randy's teammates laughed even more.

Randy: Ey Liam, is she your sister or something?
Liam: What!? No way. I guess I was acting like a windbreak to her, that's all?
Teammates: (Laughing)
Todd: (Laughing) Nice one.
Randy: That would've been humiliating, and you would have absolutely lost my vote for captain of the football team.
Liam: So, I got your vote?
Randy: And the teams'.
Liam: Cool.

Randy and his minions, I mean teammates, left Liam and Samantha.

Samantha: Wow. Windbreak...very funny.
Liam: I told you about this. I now have a high chance of being the captain.
Samantha: At the expense of your sister.
Liam: Shhhhh. Not in public and especially not at school.
Samantha: And then what after you become captain? Will I be your sister then?
Liam: Well...
Samantha: Typical...brothers (walking away).

Samantha couldn't believe that her own brother, and biological one, for that matter, was ashamed of being related to her. This world was truly something else.

One day, they went to church.

Sabrina: Wear this (giving Samantha an oversized coat).
Samantha: Why? I mean, it's so big.
Sabrina: To act like you actually have flesh.
Samantha: Are you serious?

Sabrina: What?
Samantha: Just forget it. I can just stay home you know.
Sabrina: I'm not having that. Let's just go. That looks better. Just don't remove it.
Samantha: Fine.

They got to the church.

Mary: Sabrinaaa!
Sabrina: Great. Mary!
Mary: How are... Sammy?
Samantha: (Putting her coat back on) Yes.
Mary: When I said reduce her portions, I didn't mean starve her to death.
Sabrina: Oh, that. She went on her own diet.
Craig: Mom, I locked the door. Here are the keys. Oh and I... Samantha!
Samantha: Craig.
Craig: Why do you look like a human twig?
Samantha: Excuse me?

Mary laughed and Samantha glared at her.

Mary: (Stops laughing) That's not nice Craig. Well, we better get going.

They left and got into church and Craig and his mother just laughed as they got in. Samantha could tell they were laughing at her.

Samantha: (Bitterly) Witch.
Sabrina: Samantha! That teaches you to do as I say. I told you not to remove that coat.

Weeks went by and the end of the term started rolling in.

Mr Richards: With a 96%...
Everyone: Samantha!!!
Mr Richards: What...in...the...world!

Samantha reached out for her paper.

Mr Richards: (Laughing) Wait. Hold up. (Turning cruelly serious) I am gone for a term and this. What did you do to yourself?
Samantha: (In a fragile tone) What do you mean?
Mr Richards: You are looking like a walking skeleton. I mean, are you replacing Gregory's skeletal structure?
Everyone: (Laughing)
Tony: Sir...
Mr Richards: What Tony? You know, as a good boyfriend you should tell her the truth.
Samantha: He's not my boyfriend.
Mr Richards: Oh, I see, but still, as a good friend you should be honest with her. Tell her right now that she is skinny.
Tony: I can't do that.
Everyone: Booooooo!
Mr Richards: Well you're no fun. Anyway Samantha, because of the state you are in, it forces me to reduce your mark.
Samantha: What!? But sir?
Mr Richards: But nothing. I said that psychologists have gorgeous bodies and have fat in the right places and not no fat at all. So that's 10 marks off.
Everyone: Oooo Oooo!!!
Freddy: But sir, when she was stout you reduced marks. Weren't you supposed to add since you know she was big? I mean, now she's small I understand, but when...
Mr Richards: SHUT UP FREDDY! Now (changing her grade to 86%) that will teach you that to become a

psychologist you have to also look the part (throwing the paper at her).

Samantha: (Picking up the paper) You know sir, it's not always about looks.

Mr Richards: SHUT UP! SHUT UP SAMANTHA! If you think you are going to amount to anything looking like a big bomb lollipop, a big head and a scrawny body (chuckling rottenly), then you are not living in the world we are living.

Samantha felt so violated. This man was one of the reasons a lot of women felt uncomfortable with who they were. He had such a superiority complex.

They got home and her brother, knowing very well that she had asked to show her report first, did exactly what she did not want him to do.

Samantha: Liam, you are being so unfair (trying to block Liam from getting out of the car first).

Liam: (Pushing her out of the car and onto the snow) Maybe if you had any actual weight, you would have been able to stop me.

Liam ran first into the house, leaving a mumbling and grumbling Samantha in the freezing snow, and gave their dad his report.

Kevin: Liam my boy (rubbing his back) That's my boy!

Sabrina: What's all the praise about?

Kevin: My child right here just got 7As and 3Bs.

Sabrina: Liam! (hugging him). I'm so proud. (Turning to Samantha who was brushing off the last bits of snow that she had collected from the push in the snow.) What happened to you?

Kevin: And where is your report?

Samantha: For the first question, ask Liam. For the second (gulping), I have it but I didn't do so well.
Kevin: Of course, it's not like you can produce anything. You see your child, Sabrina.
Samantha: (Taking a deep breath) Here.
Kevin: What is this?
Sabrina: What did she get? (Taking the report card from her husband.)
Kevin: 5As, 3Bs and 2Cs.
Sabrina: That's a drop. Samantha, what is going on?
Kevin: Did you think reducing your weight also meant reducing your grades? Because if so, then you are wrong young lady. This is why I just wanted sons.
Sabrina: Well, it's already too late for that. Samantha, if you see that school is now too much for you, then there is plan B. You can just waltz into a rich man's life.
Liam: Well, with that vine-like body, I doubt anyone would want her.
Kevin: You can say that again. Here's your useless report (throwing the report at her).

Samantha just left and went to her room.

Her dad had scratched her cheek with the corner of her report card when he threw the book at her. She was cleaning the scratch while, like raindrops flowing on drip tip leaves, tears flowed down her cheeks. She felt like an outcast in a place she was supposed to take as home, a place where she was supposed to feel like she belonged, a place where she was supposed to take as a shelter from all the criticisms outside, but it was so ironic to her that this was the place she actually felt was worse than the outside, a place she wished she could run away from. She looked at herself in the mirror and she started hearing all the nasty comments she had heard from the beginning of the term, and she closed her ears and threw her pillow at the mirror. She decided to write in her diary.

03/08/21

Dear Diary

This has been an awful term. Instead of feeling accepted, I felt like an outcast. People were making fun of the way I lost weight. They said I had grown skinny. They said horrible stuff like I look like I can be blown away by a gale or gust of wind, that I'm skinny, asking me if I'm able to carry pompoms, calling me a stick-man, a human stick insect, asking if I have been eating, calling me paper-thin, that I look starved and that I look like a twig. Kenzie called me unhealthy, and I couldn't get into the cheer squad. That girl Katey even broke a toothpick and said that's my future. My crush, Randy, made fun of me and asked how I was not flying away during this windy day, and my brother, who disowned me in front of them, said he was acting like my wind break. Mr Richards even humiliated me once again in class. He asked me if I had replaced our science teacher's skeletal structure. He said I look like a big bomb lollipop. He said I have a big head and scrawny body. He even reduced my mark. Worse off, I'm dropping in school and I feel miserable. My parents and my brother don't understand what's affecting me or what I'm doing. I know very well that even if I do tell them, they will say it's all in my head. I'll just have to deal with this myself and solve this myself. I'm going to work on getting the perfect body.

Hope Carter

That holiday, Samantha worked on getting the so-called "perfect body." She did everything in its right proportions, from the food she ate to the routines of workouts she did. She also upped her calories, gaining 5kg [11 lbs.]. The last term of the year, Spring season, arrived, and it was time to go back to school.

CHAPTER 3

Sabrina: Why do we do this every term? Liam! Samantha! Time!
Liam: (Running downstairs) Here!
Samantha: (Coming downstairs) Mom, could you zip me up?
Liam: Uh, Samantha.
Samantha: Yes Liam.
Liam: You look good.
Samantha: Why thank you Liam.
Sabrina: I second that. Good riddance to your skinny self.
Kevin: Still here? (Kissing Sabrina on the forehead).
Sabrina: We are just about to leave honey. I've to get Samantha...
Kevin: Samantha!
Samantha: Yes Father.
Kevin: You look different.
Sabrina: She looks perfect. I mean, the routines she did this holiday really worked. She almost looks as great as me.
Kevin: (Laughing) Well, yes dear. I'm just worried that she might indulge in things she mustn't, thinking she's a big girl, which she's not.
Samantha: Dad!!!
Kevin: Well, why else would you look the way you look?
Samantha: Um... (looking down).
Sabrina: Well, we don't have time for this. Okay, c'mon kids, let's go.

Samantha couldn't believe it. What just happened? She went to the car.

Sabrina: So, I guess we have to get you new dresses since all the other dresses are either too big or too small. Man, this year has been something else.
Samantha: You can say that again (with a sigh).
Sabrina: Well, it's obvious you're going to be part of the cheer team now.
Samantha: Yes.
Liam: We'll see about that.
Samantha: What do you mean Liam?
Liam: You don't know Kenzie very well, do you? Why don't we wait and see what she says? How about that?
Samantha: Whatever Liam.

Sabrina: Bye kids!
Samantha and Liam: (In chorus) Bye!

Samantha: Okay, go ahead.
Liam: What do you mean?
Samantha: The "drill."
Liam: Oh that. It doesn't matter anymore.
Samantha: Why? Wait a minute, I see now. You know what, I don't think you would want to walk with a sumo fighter or a stick-man for a sister. So, I guess I'll just lead the way then.
Liam: Sis!
Samantha: Shhhhh. Not in public and especially not at school.
Liam: Wow.

She was now apparently his sister just because she weighed 55kg [121 lb.]. Samantha just flicked her braids and got into the school hallways.

Tony: Welcome back Sa...
Samantha: (Smiling) Tony! What do you think?
Tony: (Rubbing his neck) Man, you look amazing.

Samantha: Really? Thanks.
Tony: Not that you didn't look amazing before.
Samantha: Here he goes again. Well, Randy is surely going to be in for a surprise. I'm totally going to the dance with him now.
Tony: (Sighing) Is this what this is all about?
Samantha: Well… and for the cheer squad, and just so that I fit in.
Tony: By feeding male fantasies instead of just being you and being liked for you.
Samantha: Tony, again, it's the world we live in.
Tony: No, again, Samantha, it's the world you want to live in.
Samantha: Not like you would understand anything.
Tony: But at least I'm not trying to be someone I'm not. There are consequences for everything we do Sam. When will you ever learn that? (Walking away from her and going to class).
Samantha: Tony! Tony!

Tony just ignored her and got to class.

She also got to class, and teacher after teacher complimented her on her "new transformation." She felt proud of herself, but when Tony's mother said there were consequences and risks to everything, she wasn't kidding.

During Lunch.

Katey: Samantha!
Samantha: Ugh! What Katey?
Katey: New look huh?
Samantha: Well yes. Thank you for noticing.
Katey: Wow, and you feel so proud of yourself, huh?
Samantha: Is that jealousy I sense? I mean, you should know better that jealousy is the ugliest trait.

Katey laughed wickedly.
Samantha: What's so funny?
Katey: I'm not jealous of you. I'm actually seeing you as a fool. Now you want to impress the guys, right?
Samantha: What!? That's not it.
Katey: Trying to get the male teacher's attention?
Samantha: What!? No.
Katey: You are such a whore. I knew it from the very start. (Whispering in her ear) Be careful of STIs.

Katey just left her there in utter shock. Was that what people were thinking of her? Is that what people thought of her? Was that what she was?

Tony: You would think they would put vanilla pudding for a change. Are you okay Sam?
Samantha: (Putting a forced smile on her face) Yes, Tony. I'm fine.
Tony: Owwkay then. Are you going for tryouts, or will you just wait for next year?
Samantha: Why wait? So, I gain or lose more kilograms. No thank you. I'm going for tryouts this Friday.
Tony: I would think you were tired of Kenzie.
Samantha: Well, she can't say no to me now. I have everything she asked for.
Tony: Riiight. So, we are on the same page, you are talking about the same Kenzie I know too, right?
Samantha: Well, duhh.
Tony: If you say so.

Samantha went with her mom to get new dresses.

Shop assistant: This is the size. We even call the size of this dress the perfect fit because it has the perfect measurements.

Sabrina: Well of course my daughter gets to wear that dress. She got it from me. We'll take it.
Samantha: The perfect fit? Why would you even name it such?
Sabrina: What's the problem, Samantha?
Samantha: I just think, you know what? Forget it.

Samantha got the dresses. These dresses really shaped her figure. On Friday she went for tryouts.

Felicia: At least this is our last time.
Tracy: (Perky tone) I'm gonna miss it.
Kenzie: Personally, I'm glad it's over.

Samantha came in with a cartwheel and front flip. She performed a whole routine to the song *Motivation* by Normani playing.

She finished with the splits.

Kenzie: (Clapping) NEXT!
Samantha: What!? Why?
Kenzie: Is it like you didn't hear me? You know what? (Taking a megaphone) NEXT!
Samantha: (Snatching the megaphone from her) Why Kenzie? I have everything you asked for. The fever for cheer (shaking her pompoms), the flair and glare (doing a backflip) and the cheer posture (showing her body). What more!?

Kenzie, Tracy and Felicia started laughing.

Samantha: What's so funny?
Kenzie: You missed my favorite pointer.
Samantha: What? Which one?
Kenzie: I... don't... like you!

Samantha: What!?
Kenzie: You think you're smart, right? Getting this stripper body so you can seduce the guys, the coach and maybe even the male teachers. That's what it is, right?
Samantha: No.
Kenzie: Then what is it for?
Samantha: Umm...
Kenzie: That's what I thought. SLUT! So, (taking the megaphone back) NEXT!!!
Samantha: (Closing her ears) Fine.

Samantha walked out feeling like roadkill. She had wanted to be in the cheer squad ever since grade 3 and that was just taken away from her. What hurt her most was the fact that it wasn't because she couldn't cheerlead but it was because of the way she looked and Kenzie's hate towards her. She went to the ladies' room to comfort herself. She locked herself in an ablution and she sniffled and wept in utter bitterness.

In the ladies' room.

Laura: Did you see what she's wearing? The uniform is literally hugging her body.
Courtney: Tell me about it. Samantha is such an attention seeker.
Laura: What is she trying to prove?
Courtney: That she can get pregnant before we all do.

Laura and Courtney just laughed.

Samantha couldn't believe what she was hearing. It seemed everyone was just shaming her for the way she looked. It broke her. When she had thought she had finally solved all her problems she had made a mess of everything. Laura and Courtney kept gossiping and insulting her until she could take it no more and she decided to come out of the ablution she was in.

Laura closed her mouth.

Courtney: Sammy, hey. How long have you been in there?
Samantha: (Washing her face) Not that long.
Laura: I have a question Samantha.
Samantha: (Looking in the mirror at them and trying not to show her face) What is it?
Laura: So, how did you get from fat to skinny to provocative?
Samantha: Exercise.
Courtney: Yea right. You definitely took some pills or injections to get to the point you are now.
Samantha: (Turning around and looking directly at them with bleeding red eyes) It's not that at all. I really just exercised.
Laura: (With a scoff) Were you seriously crying? Wow. Who's to blame? You did this to yourself princess. Now look at the consequences you have created for yourself.
Samantha: (In a whisper) I just wanted to be accepted.

Laura and Courtney laughed at her.

Samantha: Just leave me alone. (Walking out of the ladies' room).

Laura and Courtney started bullying her by pulling her hair and her clothes. She quickly ran out, tears in her eye sockets like water behind the Kariba Dam wall.
One blink and the floodgates would be opened. She got to her locker and started packing her books.

Tony: Should I say congratula...

Samantha closed her locker and looked him straight in the eyes.

Tony: Sammy, why do your eyes look dragon breath pepper red?
Samantha: Kenzie, Felicia, Tracy, Laura and Courtney. They said I look like a slut and a whore and that I got pills and injections to look like this. (She broke down). They... they even said I'm... I'm do... do... doing this for... the males. Like seriously?
Tony: Woah, slow down and calm down Sammy. Are you seriously going to listen to all those nasty comments after all you have gone through?
Samantha: You'd think I would be numb right? It still hurts though. Plus, I take everything to heart. I'm a...
Tony: ...A sensitive person. I know. I've known that forever Sam. Everything will be fine. Don't let words define who you are.
Samantha: (With a sigh) I'll come to your house for homework.
Tony: Sure.
Samantha got into her mom's car, followed by Liam.
Sabrina: How was your day, you two?
Liam: Awesome. You are looking at the new football captain.
Sabrina: Wow Liam. (Hugging him). I'm so proud of you (pinching his cheek).
Liam: Mom, stop (rubbing his cheek).
Sabrina: What of you, young lady? Am I looking at the new chee...
Samantha: No. I didn't make it.
Sabrina: Oh. Well, you can just tryout nex...
Liam: (laughing) ... I knew it. Did I not tell you so?
Samantha: You don't even know the story, so just shut up.
Liam: Even if I don't know, I know no matter how much you try you'll never make it into the cheer squad as long

as Kenzie is choosing. She hates you with a passion ever since grade three when you took the limelight and became the best gymnast.

Samantha: I said shut up Liam!

Liam: Another thing I know is that (giving her a cruel look) you're dumb, and you'll never be as good as me.

Samantha: (Throwing a book that was in her lap at Liam).

Liam: Owww. What was that for?

Samantha: Good for you, you no good, pea sized brained, egocentric narcissist.

Liam: (Taking the book that Samantha had thrown at him and he was just about to throw it).

Sabrina: Cut it out, you two!! We are going home alright, and no fighting. Do I make myself clear?

Samantha and Liam: (In chorus) Yes, ma'am.

Sabrina: Good.

Samantha couldn't believe the nerve her brother had. She blamed her father for her brother's superiority complex. He would constantly teach Liam to be a man, but a man with no self-conscious, respect or empathy for women. This is why the world would remain the way it was. If boys, especially the young, were not taught that a girl was capable of doing as much as boys could and even more, and how to treat the female species, the whole superiority complex was going to be inherited from generation to generation, which was a horrific nightmare. Imagine the number of girls, young ladies and women who would have to deal with that anytime they tried to do something. Just imagine!

Samantha then later went on to Tony's house.

Samantha: Mom, I'm going over to Tony's place. Is it okay?

Sabrina: (On her phone) Yeah, yeah, sure.

Samantha wore some white bum shorts, a red body-hugging top and some white sneakers.
She decided to walk to his house rather than be dropped off. She then regretted it. Let's see why.

Samantha was walking with her hands crossed around her chest, pondering on all the things she had been going through, when she stopped in her tracks at the sight of a guy on the corner of where she wanted to go through.

The guy seemed to be in his early to mid-20s. Puffs of smoke went up in the air from smoking a cigarette. He wore a black hoodie, black jeans and black sneakers. She argued with herself on whether or not to go past the guy or to just turn around and go back home. She was so fearful. The thought of going through was heavy, but the thought of going back was heavier so she decided to go through. She made an oath with herself that she wasn't going to draw his attention or draw attention to herself but, oh well, that was all futile because the moment she passed through, he put up his head and stared at her. She avoided any eye contact with him, but even still, she could feel his eyes staring at her from the back, which gave her shivers down her spine.

All of a sudden, she started hearing footsteps as if someone was following her. She decided to walk faster, and the footsteps got faster. She then began to jog, and the footsteps began to jog too. She decided to run and the footsteps behind her started running. In terror, she turned back to see who it was and, not to her surprise, it was that fella who she had passed on the corner. Her heart beat like the drums of an award-winning orchestra as she tried to outrun him.

Unfortunately for Samantha, but fortunately for that guy, she wasn't an athlete, and he caught up to her. He put his hand on her mouth and grabbed her arms with the other. The grip was that of a koala on its branch, inseparable. Her heart sank like the titanic at the bottom of the sea. Samantha started crying, afraid of the unknown, afraid of this putrid stranger's intentions. What did he want with her? What did he want to do to her? What was going to happen next?

Stranger: (Whispering in her ear) Shhhhh. Shhhhh. Shhhhh. Hush now love. I just want to talk.

Droplets rolled from her eyes to the rough palm of the stranger which was on her mouth.

Stranger: Don't cry. Shhh. Shhh.

Samantha was only left with three gates to get to her destination, but she could neither scream nor even make a screech to gain someone's attention so as to save her. No one walked in or out of their yard. "For what reason?" they would respond to anyone who asked them why, it was such a quiet place. The people were so secretive. Tony's hood was the noiseless type. It was for the middle class to rich class people. His mother was a manager of a company that dealt with real estate. Tony's neighborhood explained why Tony was such a calm and chilled person. On a more serious note, Samantha was in a life-threatening situation, and she needed to get out of it and fast. She stopped crying and thought of what she could do.

Stranger: That's it baby. Relax.

Samantha took this opportunity when the guy was also relaxing his grip on her, thinking she was loosening up to kick his shin with her heel. When he removed his hands off her, she kicked him where "the sun don't shine."

Stranger: (Bitterly) Why you little...

Samantha ran as fast as she could to the gate, banged it with all her might and pressed the intercom continuously. He started walking towards her, slowly dragging himself in pain. Tony heard the ruckus that was going on and quickly ran to the gate.

Tamika: Tony Goodness Brown. Where do you think you are off to without answering the intercom? For all we know, it could be a thief.
Tony: It's Sammy. She told me she was just around the corner, and Mom, what did I say about calling me Goodness? I really dislike that name.
Tamika: Well, blame your father, who left us and left you with that name as a second name. Why the banging?
Tony: Maybe she's in trouble. Let me go.
Tamika: Tony!! That kid (going to answer the intercom). Yes, who is it?
Samantha: Heeellp!!! It's Sammy. Please!!!
Tamika: Sammy!!

Meanwhile, Tony had started opening the gate and his mother followed after him.

Tony: Sammy!
Samantha: Tony. Thank God.

The stranger then grabbed her arm, and she held on to the gate while he pulled her. Tony grabbed her other arm when she was slipping and it was like a tug of war.
Tony was losing his grip as the stranger was older and stronger. Luckily, Tony's mom had brought a belt and smacked the stranger right across the face. He whined like a dog that had been beaten with a metal strap and took off, running away. Samantha went straight into Tony's arms and started crying.

Tony: It's okay Sam. You're okay now.
Tamika: (Hugging the two) Are you two okay?
Tony: Yes. Thanks Mom.
Tamika: Sam?

Samantha was nodding her head and hugging Tony's mom too.

Tamika: Let's get in.

She locked the gate and took Samantha and her son inside where it was safe.

Samantha: (Stuttering) I…I…can't believe…that.
Tamika: (Rubbing her back) It's okay dear. Don't cry.
Tony: (Rubbing her hands) You're safe here.
Tamika: Why didn't you let your parents drop you off?
Samantha: (Sniffling) I…I wanted to clear my thoughts.
Tamika: What thoughts?
Samantha: People at school are calling me a whore, a slut and all that stuff.
Tamika: Oh Samantha. I told you about this. Everything has consequences.
Samantha: Well, there's nothing I can do now.
Tony: She's right. She'll have to deal with this type of life now.
Tamika: It's going to be okay, love. Just be strong. I mean, you look absolutely beautiful.
Tony: (Wiping her tears off her face) She's not lying Sammy.
Samantha: You two are right. I have dealt with so much. I can deal with this.

Samantha spent some time with them, talking, laughing and feeling like she was actually part of a family.

Samantha: Well, unfortunately I have to go, otherwise I'll miss my curfew.

Tony: I'll walk you home.
Samantha: Yes please.
Tamika: Well, bye sweetheart.
Samantha: Bye, Mom (giving her a hug).

Tony walked her home.

Samantha: Thank you, Tony. What did I do to deserve a best friend like you?
Tony: I wonder.
Samantha: Well, I'll see you at church on Sunday.
Tony: Absolutely, and where's my hug?
Samantha: (Smiling). Tony. Here you go (giving him a hug). Bye Tony.
Tony: Bye Sam.

They went to church on Sunday

Sabrina: I can't wait for that brat Mary to see you now. You might have been fat then skinny, but now... now you look like a model, like me.
Samantha: Oh, you've gotta be kidding me.
Sabrina: What?
Samantha: (With a sigh). Forget it.
Mary: Oh, Sabrina darling!
Sabrina: Mary!
Mary: How are...oh my gosh...Samantha?
Samantha: Hi Mrs Robinson.
Mary: Why you look like a bad bit...
Craig: ...Mom here you.... Samantha, is that you?
Samantha: Yes Craig.
Craig: Well, that's more like it.
Samantha: What's more like it?
Craig: Your body. You look like a normal 17-year-old now.

Samantha: Is that a sexist statement? Are you implying I was abnormal before?
Sabrina: Okay now. Well, Mary, she worked out and it paid off. She looks like me.
Mary: Well, I guess. Just make sure she controls her desires, if you know what I mean? C'mon now Craig.
Craig: Sure Mom. (To Samantha) I'll get your number later.

He ran after his mom, who was already entering the church.

Samantha: (Speaking to herself). What about no.
Sabrina: Man, that Mary is a witch.
Samantha: You didn't believe me when I said it.

After a few weeks passed the school decided to introduce a rule to allow the school children to wear casuals and not school uniforms so that they could enjoy the last weeks of their term. One day Samantha went to school wearing black ripped jeans and a red body-hugging top when she had an encounter with Randy.

Samantha: (Closing her locker). Woah, you startled me Randy.
Randy: I didn't mean to. I just couldn't help but be so moved by how you look these days. You look gorgeous.
Samantha: Thank you Randy.
Randy: Which means we can be what you wanted now (drawing closer to her to give her a kiss).
Samantha: What!? Woah. Slow your role man.
Randy: What is it? Isn't this what you wanted?
Samantha: Who told you such?
Randy: Well it's obvious. You reduced your weight for me and got this smoking hot body for me. That's what girls do. They get bodies like yours to impress guys like us. Girls like you deserve to be with guys like me.

Samantha: So, let me get this straight you think I got like this for you, and you like me now because of my looks, and you just want us to be together without getting to know who I really am?
Randy: Well...if you say it like that, it sounds...
Samantha: ...SICK! That's what it sounds like.
Randy: Excuse me?
Samantha: You know what? I'm not having this. I never liked you, don't like you and never will. Got it, Randy Sullivan. (With that, Samantha flipped her braids and went to class).
Randy: Whatever. I don't care. Go. It's not like I liked you. You aren't that pretty anyway. You are the one who is losing out.

Samantha just walked away with her head up high, and every bit of like, love, attraction and infatuation was like ice in the summer heat, non-existent. She didn't care about him anymore and most probably never would.

One Saturday, her mom decided to go buy clothes with her. Samantha wore a white crop top hoodie, grey shredded jeans and white sneakers.

Samantha: I'm ready.
Sabrina: What are you wearing?
Samantha: Clothes.
Sabrina: Ha ha ha. Well, you are not going out looking like that. I mean, your look is screaming, "rape me please!" Go change into something more modest and decent, not provocative.
Samantha: Wow. (Talking to herself) She called me fat, then skinny, and now I'm provocative. What does this woman want?

Samantha changed and wore plain grey jeans and a white tuck-in top with white sneakers.

One would wonder why her mother had little to almost no empathy for Samantha. Samantha had 3 theories for this. The first theory was that it had to do with how her dad treated her mom. He had a tendency to demean her and make her feel small. As a result of this her mother reflected the same treatment to Samantha, just to basically let out her frustration.

The second theory was to do with how society had brainwashed her to believe that it was always the woman's fault in every situation, thus leading to her being so critical towards Samantha.

The third theory was one that was painful to swallow but could have been the reason. Samantha believed that her mother had never actually wanted a girl and that Samantha being born was not something her mother was at all happy about, worse off with the fact that Liam was literally the golden child and she was somewhat the defective child. Denzel Washington did once say it that, "A mother is a son's first true love. A son, especially their first son, is a mother's last true love."

Despite all these theories, though, Samantha knew her mother loved her. She just did not show it enough.

When they got into the shop the guy at the counter stared at Samantha for a straight 60 seconds. Of course, this made poor Samantha super uncomfortable such that there was a moment when she turned back to see his eyes glued on her. Her mom decided to get deeper into the store. You would think she got lucky but that guy decided to follow them or rather her. He started pretending to fix some clothes behind them. Samantha started getting anxious and her heart started beating faster. She felt like she was losing her breath.

Samantha: Um, Mom, are you done yet?
Sabrina: What? No, not yet. Why?
Samantha: I just wanted to go back home.
Sabrina: Are you serious? Kids like you need to get out more often. You are always glued to those screens of yours. Be it your phones or your laptops.
Samantha: (With a sigh) Fine (crossing her arms).
Sabrina: You know you can help me with getting to know how much this dress costs.

The guy must have heard them and went back to the counter.

Samantha: (Nervously) Me?
Sabrina: (Sarcastically) No, Kim Kardashian. Yes, you Samantha Hope Carter. Go over to the young man over there and ask the price because there is no price tag on this.
Samantha: (Nervously) Where?
Sabrina: To the counter over there.
Samantha: (Nervously) To who?
Sabrina: Samantha!
Samantha: Right, right. To that guy who's most likely in his early 20s. Can't you just go?
Sabrina: Who do you think you are talking to?
Samantha: Sorry Mom.
Sabrina: Yea now go. You are the one who wants to go back home, right? So you're wasting time. You know if I had come with Liam, he would be confident and active and not complain so much.
Samantha: (With a sigh) Of course.

Samantha then got the itty-bitty courage inside her to go over to the guy.

Samantha: Um, excuse me. How much is this?
Guy: Oh, hey beautiful.
Samantha: Sorry. My bad. Hi. So how much...
Guy: My name is Travis, by the way, and you are?
Samantha: Uhh... Rosah.
Travis: That's an absolute lie. I heard your mom calling you Samantha.
Samantha: So why did you ask if you already knew then?
Travis: (Slyly smiling). Confirmation.
Samantha: Owwkay then. How much is this?
Travis: Give me.

Samantha gave him the dress, and even though he kept constant eye contact with her, she drifted away.

Travis: May I have your number?
Samantha: I don't have a phone (her phone rang).
Travis: Really? Doesn't sound like it.
Samantha: My mom's phone.
Travis: Righht?
Samantha: How much?
Travis: $35. (Going around the counter to where she was). You're a bad liar.
Samantha: The dress.
Travis: What's in it for me?
Samantha: Nothing. I just want the dress.
Travis: (Drawing very close to her) C'mon now. (Whispering in her ear) There has to be something.
Sabrina: Samantha!
Samantha: Coming! The dress.
Travis: Saved by your mom (giving her the dress).
Samantha: You're messed up.
Travis: Well, you have to expect it if you dress like a bad bit...
Sabrina: ...Samantha!
Samantha: Coming! Whatever Travis.

Samantha went back with the dress to her mom.

Sabrina: What was taking you so long?
Samantha: It was that guy. You won't believe the ner...
Sabrina: ...Wow. Typical. You were flirting with him instead of doing what I had sent you to do.
Samantha: No. It's not that at all. He was...
Sabrina: ...Save it Samantha. I know how you teens are, and ever since you got that body you have been acting all grown up. Your dad was so right. Don't forget it's so easy to become a mother at your age, and it's not at all worth it.
Samantha: But...
Sabrina: How much is that dress?
Samantha: Mom...
Sabrina: How much is that dress!?
Samantha: $35.
Sabrina: Next time I'll know to come with Liam instead of you (snatching the dress from Samantha).

They bought a few dresses for her mom, and they went home. In the car, Samantha sat in the passenger seat feeling like a victim of her emotions. If only she had heard her out. If she only understood how she felt. If only she understood what she was going through. Unfortunately, she would never understand and would never hear her out. That's the way it was. This was the world she lived in.

One day they were given their results for a pop quiz that they had in Literature.

Mr Richards: The highest with a 96%...
Everyone: Samantha!!!
Mr Richards: Of cour... Wow. Samantha, is that you?

Samantha: Yes sir.
Mr Richards: (Fixing his spectacles) That's a true psychologist's body right there.
Samantha: Uh, thank you (reaching out to take her paper).
Mr Richards: You know what?
Samantha: What?
Mr Richards: You deserve an extra 2 marks.
Samantha: Oh uh, no. That won't be fair.
Everyone: Uhhhh!!! Noooooo!!!
Mr Richards: SHUT IT! Yes, where was I? Right, your extra 2 marks.
Samantha: (Hesitating) Ummm, thank you sir.

There was another time once again when she was supposed to present at assembly.

Principal Penolopy: For the weather report, Samantha Carter.

Everyone applauded

Not surprisingly she made her way to the stage, she could feel her voice slipping away and the trembling in her knees. She started hearing all that delusional laughter of people laughing at her and mocking her for getting the so-called "perfect body." Once again, she just couldn't do it. Anxiety was crippling her.

Samantha: (Looking down) I can't, Principal Penolopy.
Principal Penolopy: Oh c'mon, again, um…
Everyone: Huh?

Samantha just left the stage and the hall.

Principal: Well, the weather for today is going to be…

After assembly in class.
Katey: Wow. Three times, the attention seeker couldn't present. How disgraceful.
Tony: Ignore her Sam.
Samantha: (Nodding her head with a sigh.)

Weeks went by and Mr Richards just acted super weird. She started avoiding him, and he started noticing this so he made a plan that would ensure that she would come to him. Her grades started dropping, and even when she got everything marked correctly, he would give her a low percentage. Mr Richards' plan worked, and one day after class she went to him.

Mr Richards: And with an 88%, the highest is…
Everyone: Sa…
Mr Richards: …Nope. It's Katey.
Everyone: Huh!?
Katey: Yess (looking at Samantha and sticking out her tongue).

Samantha couldn't believe it. She'd had a streak of being the best in Literature. Now Katey was the best. What mostly shocked her was when she looked through her paper, once again her percentage was not adding up to the number of ticks. She had to ask him what was wrong.

Mr Richards: Samantha! Is everything okay?
Samantha: Well, actually, it's about my percentage…
Mr Richards: Yea, you really have to pull up. I mean 86%. Not the Sammy I know.
Samantha: Yea, but it's not adding up.
Mr Richards: Oh really. You don't say?
Samantha: Yes. See.
Mr Richards: Mmmm. Oh, I see. Why don't you come to me just before you go home?

Samantha: Absolutely. Thank you.
Mr Richards: Anytime.

When she left, his eyes followed her all the way to the door. When lessons were over, she decided to go and see him.

Tony: So, you are going to Mr Richards?
Samantha: Well, it's not like I have a choice. My marks aren't adding up. Why?
Tony: He's acting…I don't know…a little off around you lately.
Samantha: (Laughing) What!? You're kidding right?
Tony: (Looking at her plainly.)
Samantha: Wait, you're serious? Oh, c'mon Tony. He's a grown man with a wife and 2 kids.
Tony: Remember he has stories of his own.
Samantha: Like the rumors that have to do with him having other kids with different women and raping 3 girls? Please, Tony. It's just people trying to tarnish his image.
Tony: And yet he is the same person who has fat-shamed you, skinny-shamed you and has been a bit too nice to you lately.
Samantha: Oh, so that's what it's all about. If you call reducing my percentage nice, then I don't think you know what being nice is all about.
Tony: I'm just saying, be careful.
Samantha: Everything is going to be okay Tony. Okay?

Samantha went to class, where he said he would meet her.

Mr Richards: Sammy! (Standing up and giving her an awkward hug.)
Samantha: Uh, sir, you're hugging me.
Mr Richards: Well I thought I just, you know never mind, soo what seems to be the problem?

Samantha: (Diverting her gaze and looking aside) Right. My marks aren't adding up to my percentage.

Mr Richards: Why don't you take a seat in that chair over there? The one in the middle.

Samantha: Umm, It's fine. I'll just stand. So...

Mr Richards: ...Otherwise (removing his specs). I just won't help you.

Samantha: Fine, fine, I'll sit down.

Mr Richards: Okay then. Now, what is the problem?

Samantha: Recently my grades have been dropping, but I have been noticing that my marks are... what are you doing, Mr Richards?

Mr Richards: Just massaging your shoulders.

Samantha: For what?

Mr Richards: So that you calm down.

Samantha: Sir, stop (shrugging her shoulders to get rid of his hands).

Mr Richards: What is it?

Samantha: You're making this seem weird.

Mr Richards: My bad. I didn't mean to make this weird.

Samantha: It's fine.

Mr Richards: You know what, from now on I'll give you 98% and anything above.

Samantha: Sir, that doesn't make sense. It's not right.

Mr Richards: You're right. It will be suspicious. I'll give you 92% and above then.

Samantha: Sir!!

Mr Richards: You can just call me Bad Boy Richie, Sammy, no need for formality.

Samantha: Bad bo...What!? No!

Mr Richards: What do you want then!?

Samantha: Fair marks that's all.

Mr Richards: Ohhh. You should have just said so. I can make that happen if you help me out. If you know what I mean?

Samantha: What!? Mr Richards! I am not that kinda girl.

Mr Richards: Oh please. With the black yoga pants and hot pink tank top. You are obviously trying to draw male attention.

Samantha: No, I'm not. Why do men think we dress for them and why can't men just look at girls and women as human beings and not objects to take advantage of?

Mr Richards: Well, that's why you shouldn't wear such tight clothes or revealing clothes or body shaping outfits. It's your fault men are the way they are. Women draw men's lust.

Samantha: So, a grown man can't control himself. This world will never change if we keep making excuses. (Standing up) I'm leaving. You obviously don't want to genuinely help me and you obviously want to help with an ulterior motive.

Mr Richards: You're not going anywhere (grabbing her arm like an officer grabbing a criminal in custody and glaring at her with serial killer eyes) You think you are so smart, huh? I can easily hurt you Samantha.

Samantha had been grabbed so tightly that she could not even fidget. Fear spread like a veld fire throughout her body, afraid of what Mr Richards was going to do. Luckily Tony had been waiting by the glass door ever since she sat on the chair and had seen Mr Richards weird behaviour from the constant checking her out to massaging her shoulders until that very moment. When he saw him grabbing Samantha's arm, he knew something was not right and decided to barge in.

Tony: Oh, my bad. I was looking for Samantha.

Mr Richards: (Removing his hand and wearing his specs) And why is that, Tony? Didn't she tell you she would be with me?

Tony: Oh yeah. I must have forgotten. Her mom is waiting for her.
Mr Richards: I see. She was actually leaving.
Tony: Okay Sammy let's get going.
Samantha: (Rolling her eyes at Mr Richards) I'm coming.

Tony left with a cross-armed Samantha and they got to an empty parking lot.

Samantha: Where's my mom?
Tony: I lied to get you out of there.
Samantha: I see. Go ahead. Just say it.
Tony: You know how badly I want to say that, but I'm not going to. Are you alright though?
Samantha: (Wiping a tear that had formed on her left cheek) Yea. We should go home.
Tony: Sure. I'll walk you home.

Tony walked her home, and he went to his mom's house afterwards. Samantha couldn't believe it. Mr Richards was such a male chauvinist, a misogynist and such a pervert.
From that day on Mr Richards started giving her the lowest marks even when she would correctly answer all the questions in the paper. Later on that term, a party was hosted.

Tony: Are you going?
Samantha: I don't know if my parents will allow me to go to a late-night party.
Tony: I'll go with you. To make sure you're "safe."
Samantha: (Sarcastically) Oh my. My knight in shining armor.
Tony: (Sarcastically) Ha ha Samantha Hope Carter.
Samantha: I obviously would go with you but they would want Liam to go too. Since they trust Liam and he will control me and prevent me from indulging in things "I'm not ready for yet."

Tony: What? So, they don't trust you?
Samantha: They trust Liam. That's all I know.
Tony: Wow. Your parents are really something.
Samantha: You can say that again.
Tony: Your parents are really something.
Samantha: (Smiling) Tony.

When they got home, Samantha decided to try her luck.

Samantha: Uhh Mom.
Sabrina: What is it Samantha?
Samantha: Can I go to a party on Saturday?
Sabrina: It's okay. Wait a minute (getting off her phone). What time does this party start and end, because if it's the one that is from 6pm till late then you...
Samantha: ...are out of my mind. I know, but Mom, if it was Liam you were going to say it's okay.
Sabrina: Well of course. He's a guy and can protect himself, and even if he sleeps with a girl, it's not evident.
Samantha: Wow, Mom, so you are actually encouraging him to sleep with innocent girls. This is why I wanted to go for self-defense lessons and do you know what you said when I asked?
Sabrina: Well I...
Samantha: ...said no, Mom. You said, "No, what for? You'll be protected by your brother and boyfriend." You don't even want me to be independent and strong. You term that masculine and not feminine.
Sabrina: Samantha!!!

At that very moment, Liam and her dad entered the room.

Kevin: Woah. Is everything okay in here?
Sabrina: No. Your daughter here wants (Samantha signaled to her mom not to say anything) to go to a late-night party.

Kevin: A late-night party? To do what? Lose your virginity Samantha?
Samantha: NO! I'm so sick of you both thinking that's all I want. There's more to the world than that. Argh!
Kevin: Don't give us an attitude Samantha.
Samantha: Sorry. I really want to go to that party.
Liam: Wait, is it the Saturday one? Dad just gave me permission to go.
Kevin: Is that the one?
Samantha: Yes.
Kevin and Sabrina: (In chorus) Well, you can go then.
Sabrina: As long as Liam goes.
Samantha: (Mumbling in anger.)
Sabrina: You can either go or stay here with us.
Samantha: I'll go.
Liam: I'll drop you there.
Samantha: No wayy. I don't want to be seen with you.
Kevin: Samantha!
Samantha: No way. I know why he wants me to go with him, and I'm not having it.
Liam: So, how will you get there?
Samantha: Tony will pick me up and drop me off back here. *Comprende.*
Liam: (Shrugging) Your choice.

Samantha had posted a picture on Instagram 3 days before, and she was wearing a body-hugging red dress. She checked the comments, and she regretted doing so. There were such crude and raw comments.

These were some of them:

"Man! Girl, your body looks appetizing."
"She's not only a snack but a whole meal. When can I come over, shawty?"

"You look like a whore."
"Now you are a slut. Who do you want to seduce?"
"From fat to skinny to stripper. People will do anything for attention."
"Someone wants to get preg so soon."
"You're an attention seeker."
"I can be your sugar daddy if you want."

There were more disgusting comments. There were comments that could make your jaw drop in shock. It was incriminating. Unfortunately, people always have something to say.
The day of the party arrived and Tony picked her up. Samantha wore a short white jumpsuit and white sneakers with a white headband.

Tony: You look like an angel.
Samantha: Thank you, Tony.
Kevin: Make sure she's home by 9pm sharp.
Tony: Yes sir.

They got to the party. They sat together and talked and laughed. For the first time in a while, she was happy, actually happy. Little did she know she was going to be the protagonist of a horror movie. Randy saw Samantha, and Samantha saw Randy. Samantha just rolled her eyes and kept her focus on Tony. Randy was now pushed to the edge of his nerves and planned revenge. He told Todd his plan and he agreed to help him out.

Todd: Sam (nodding his head to her). Ey Tiny.
Tony: It's Tony.
Todd: Right. My fault, my fault. Uhhhh, could you come here for a sec? I need assistance with something.
Tony: With what?
Todd: C'mon dude. Help a guy out.

Samantha: Just go. I'll be right here.
Tony: I'll be back as soon as I can. Okay.

Tony left her alone, and after a few moments Randy appeared.

Randy: Samantha Carter.
Samantha: (Turning around) Randy Sullivan. I should have known these were your works.
Randy: Whatever do you mean?
Samantha: Todd coming to take Tony. Smooth. What's in store for me now?

Tony noticed Randy talking to Samantha across the room and was just about to go where they were when Todd grabbed him.

Todd: Dude, where do you think you're going?
Tony: To Samantha.
Todd: Don't you trust her?
Tony: I trust her, but I don't trust him.
Todd: Trusting her is enough Tony. She can handle herself, unless you don't think so?
Tony: I trust her. (He sighed.)

Meanwhile

Randy: Oh that, guilty. I needed to talk to you alone. I just wanted to apologize for the way I treated you this past year. It was completely uncalled for. (His ocean eyes looked so merciful.)
Samantha: Do you really mean that?
Randy: (Crossing his fingers behind his back) I'm sincerely sorry.
Samantha: Well, uh. It's okay. Let's just put it in our past.
Randy: Let me go get you some punch and we can make a toast to our reconciliation.

Samantha: Alright then.

Tony then saw him again leaving Samantha, and he smiled and continued helping Todd with the cables. Randy got their punch, and he put roofies, aka flunitrazepam (Rohypnol), in her punch. This drug was meant to knock Samantha out. He then took the punch to Samantha.

Randy: (Raising his glass shot) To reconciliation.
Samantha: To reconciliation.

They clinked their glass shots of punch, and as they both slurped their drinks, a sly smile spread across Randy's face.

Tony saw Randy and Samantha once again finishing their shots of punch. Tony still felt uneasy but tried distracting himself with the cables he was unknotting.

After a few minutes, Samantha started becoming weak; the roofies were starting to relax her muscles, exactly what Randy wanted. He decided to put one arm of hers around his neck and carried her upstairs to a bedroom, where he laid her on the bed. Tony then looked up once again. His conscience was not settled to see no Samantha and no Randy.

Tony: Dang it. I knew it.
Todd: Where do you think you are going? To disturb Randy and Samantha?

Tony then clenched his fist and punched him right in the face. Everyone just stared at him, and he, with no care in the world, just walked away and went upstairs.
The music continued, it was *Traitor* by Olivia Rodrigo. He went upstairs to the room where Randy had taken Samantha. He found it and slowly sneaked in.

Randy was slipping the second strap from her shoulder, and she was mumbling words for him not to do what he was about to do. Tony then punched him straight in the face and started kicking him and brutally beating him up. He then put him in the bathroom and locked him in. He fixed Samantha's straps and helped her out of the room and took her to his car. He drove her back home. He was lucky that the parents were not around and he got her to her bedroom. He dropped her off at 8pm. He wrote a note to her telling her that he would be there by 9am to see if she was alright.

The next day she woke up to the note that Tony had written and she totally broke down. She stayed in her room until Tony came to see her. When Tony arrived, he went to her room and sat next to her on the bed.

Tony: How are you feeling today?
Samantha: Fine. Tony?
Tony: Yes Samantha.
Samantha: Did that really happen yesterday?
Tony: Yes. I'm so sorry.
Samantha: No Tony. I'm sorry. Sorry for putting you in such a situation.
Tony: I did that for you Samantha. I'll do anything to protect you, so you don't need to apologize (he hugged her).
Samantha: (Hugging him and crying.)
Tony: It's okay. It's okay.

When Tony left after comforting her, she couldn't believe how close she was to losing her virginity, to who, to a guy who had apologized to her just before. She thought about how her white clothing was such a symbol of her innocence and dignity. Randy removing her straps was a symbol of just how easy it was to take away the virginity of a girl like her. If it wasn't for Tony, it was a thought that made her shudder. Why did he care about her so much? Why was he always there for her? Why did he protect her so much?

17/09/21

Dear Diary

I thought getting this body was all it took, but it's the exact opposite. I've been slut shamed, sexualized, been sexually assaulted and close to being raped. I literally was just making my way to Tony's place when this man chased me and grabbed me. God knows what he was going to do to me. I can't take this anymore. It's just too much to bear. I don't feel good in my own skin, the skin I was born in, the body I was given by God. My parents have told me how my body is a male attraction. People like Katey and Kenzie have said I'm a slut and that I want to seduce the male species. Randy almost raped me. Mr Richards sexually assaulted me, and now my grades are dropping because of him. This is a living nightmare. I think it's best I just hide my body, hide myself. It's way easier and safer.

Samantha Carter

CHAPTER 4

From that day onwards, she wore oversized and baggy clothing to hide herself. When Randy and Todd saw her, they growled like dogs and then saw Tony and whimpered just like the dogs they were.

Samantha avoided a lot of people and was only close to Tony. She didn't want to deal with any problems.

She then grew close to girl by the name of Mabel Sketcher. They did projects as a trio and, at times, just the two of them. They grew super close, or maybe just a bit too close. One day, when they were playing basketball at the courts together.

Samantha: I'm going to score this.
Mabel: I bet you won't.

When Samantha tried scoring, Mabel blocked it and, as it came down, they both grabbed the ball and had eye contact. Mabel then closed in and kissed her on the lips. Samantha could not believe it, but for some reason, being a Christian and all, it was bad but felt so good.

Mabel: (Grabbing the basketball) See you tomorrow, Sam.
Samantha: Uhhhh. Yea....No I mean... Uhm...
Mabel: Bye.
Samantha: Bye...bye Mabel.

Samantha was sitting on a bench when Tony arrived.

Tony: Sammy.
Samantha: (With a sigh) Hey Tony.
Tony: You look flustered.
Samantha: Something just happened.
Tony: What? (Sitting next to her.)
Samantha: I just had my first kiss.
Tony: Huh, sorry what!? With who!?
Samantha: Mabel.
Tony: Mabel who!?
Samantha: Tony! Who else?
Tony: How?
Samantha: She pecked my lips.
Tony: Owwkay.
Samantha: Yea. (Biting her bottom lip.)
Tony: Why are you acting nervous then, or are you just trying to remember the kiss you just had?
Samantha: Tony! Wait, how do you know I'm nervous?
Tony: You bite your lip or play around with your hands when you get nervous.
Samantha: Really? (Looking at her hands, which she had been playing with) Wow. Well yeah, I'm nervous. I mean, I just kissed my best friend who's, I don't know, a girl!
Tony: (Mumbling) And I thought I was going to give you your first kiss.
Samantha: What was that?
Tony: Oh nothing. So, did you, um, like it?
Samantha: Well, I... um, I... guess.
Tony: Wow. But how and why her and not any other, I don't know, another guy perhaps.
Samantha: Because guys are lame, and all guys want from a girl is her virginity and not her personality. It's different with a girl because she's genuinely into

> me, and I'm into her. Girls are just the best, and besides, there is no guy who likes me or who will ever like me.

Tony: BUT I DO! You know what? Forget it (looking away). Wow. I mean, it's your choice.

Samantha: (Hugging Tony) For a moment there, I thought you were going to judge me. You know, to be honest, I thought I had feelings for her, but I was scared and I wasn't sure, but I'm certain now. I love Mabel.

Tony took Samantha home and she would not stop bragging about Mabel. After he dropped her off, in her room, she lay on her bed upside down and just started fantasizing about Mabel and their kiss. She then put on her headphones and started listening to *I Kissed a Girl* by Katy Perry but the Nightcore Version.

Tony went to his mom and told her everything.

Tamika: Are you serious? She's considering being lesbian?

Tony: Yea. Well, with what she told me. If only she knew how much I loved her, how much I still do, and how she's hurting me.

Tamika: You should tell her.

Tony: Not now. She's made her decision. Maybe she'll change her mind.

Tamika: Nawww Tony. I know it hurts, but as a good Christian, love her, and loving her means tolerating, which means not judging her even if it puts you on the edge or in an uncomfortable position. Just respect her decision, okay? Don't forget to pray for her.

Tony: I'll just tell her God doesn't accept this, but He loves her.

Tamika: Exactly. Don't condemn her.

Tony: Yes Mom. Thank you.

Tamika: I love you.

Tony: I love you too.

Tony told Samantha what his mom had told him to say to her. She was obviously a bit defensive, but she did not disregard him or his words because she knew he was just looking out for her. Days and weeks went by and Samantha and her girlfriend, Mabel, were definitely a power couple. Though their relationship was kept on the low, they enjoyed each moment they spent with one another. Life was going great for the
two of them. That is until...

They went to church one Sunday.

Sabrina: Samantha! You're the one delaying all of us.
Samantha: Sorry, I was just talking to Mabel.
Sabrina: You and that girl?
Samantha: Mom!
Sabrina: And what are you wearing?

Samantha was wearing some grey, baggy sweatpants with a grey, baggy t-shirt and a black cap.

Samantha: What's wrong with what I'm wearing?
Sabrina: You look like a guy.
Samantha: Well I like this style Mom!
Sabrina: Fine, but the cap. Nooo. Lose the cap.
Samantha: Argh. Fine (removing the cap and stuffing it in her
 mom's purse). Let's get going.

They got to church and, before they got into the church building, she talked to Mabel. Tony joined them and they all went inside together. The sermon that day talked about the LGBTQ society.

Pastor: I say No! I say No! I say, I say No!

Everyone except Samantha, Mabel, Tamika and Tony: Yes!!!

Pastor: How can a girl be attracted to a girl? How can a boy be attracted to a boy? How can a girl be attracted to a girl and a boy? How can a boy be attracted to both a boy and a girl?

Everyone: Go deeper, pastor! Preach!

Pastor: I say such people should burn in hell. You are a woman and should be with a man, and you are a man and you should be with a woman! Can I get an Amen?

Everyone except Samantha, Mabel, Tamika and Tony: Amen!!!

Pastor: If you see any people like this, tell them that they are disgusting and wretched beings. Don't be afraid to tell them that they're going to hell because that's, of course, where they're going. You are a mini God and so have the authority to judge them.

Everyone except Samantha, Mabel, Tamika and Tony: Yess!!

Pastor: Sodom and Gomora were destroyed for such disgusting behavior. It's unacceptable! It's disgraceful! It's shameful!

Everyone except Samantha, Mabel, Tamika and Tony: Yess!! Amen!! Preach Pastor!! (Some people were clapping and making responsive noises.)

Pastor: It's devilish. If there are any lesbians, gay people, bisexuals, transgenders, or queer people, tell yourself you're a demon and are going straight to hell. Stand up everybody if you are against this custom. Stand up I say!!!

Everyone except Samantha and Mabel stood up: Yess! Wooooo!!! Amen Pastor!!

Tony and his mom had hesitated at first but ended up standing up. Samantha looked at him and Tony just looked down. Samantha then looked at Mabel, who was on the brink of bursting into tears. Samantha then slowly but hesitantly stood up, and as she did so, tears strolled down her cheeks. She couldn't believe what was happening and what she was hearing. Everything was just crumbling. Was this Pastor telling the truth? Was she going to hell if she kept dating Mabel? Mabel didn't stand up, but it crushed her to see her girlfriend stand up as well. Samantha was betraying her. Were all the moments and times they shared meaningless? Did the kisses they'd had mean nothing? What did she mean when she stood up? Was this the end of their relationship?

The service came to an end.

Sabrina: Pastor, today you really preached.
Pastor: I just say it how I see it.
Sabrina: This generation is the one with the problem. I mean, why would you fall in love with the same sex? It's preposterous.
Pastor: You can say that again. Samantha, is that you?
Samantha: (In almost a whisper and looking down) Yes pastor.
Pastor: You know, proper girls wear dresses, skirts and not these sweatpants. They are for boys.
Samantha: But pastor, sweatpants are for both boys and girls. They are just like tops.
Pastor: Then why wear oversized clothing?
Samantha: For comfort.
Pastor: Nonsense! You should wear clothing that portrays your figure, not this. Next time wear something feminine. Otherwise you'll end up liking girls instead of boys.
Sabrina: (Laughing) Oh Pastor, you're so funny. As if that would ever happen.
Pastor: (Laughing) As if.

Samantha just walked away and went to where Tony and his mom were.

Tamika: Are you alright love?
Samantha: (Nodding her head.)
Tony: I'm sorry about that.
Tamika: That Pastor was not being fair. We are taught in the Bible to love our neighbors as we love ourselves. That means no to judgment and even to people who don't share the same opinions as we do because, to be honest, we don't know what one is going thr...
Sabrina: ... Oh, shut it Tamika. So are you encouraging it?
Tamika: No Sabrina, but we have no right to condemn a person or say they are going to hell or heaven.
Sabrina: (Laughing) Don't be a fool Tamika. What the Pastor says is right.
Tamika: Don't let a mere human being define what God's word is or who He is for you. It's not bad to hear from other people, but don't be controlled by a human being but by God. Mark 12, verse 31 talks about loving your neighbor. It does not specify to love your Christian neighbor, love your black neighbor or love your straight neighbor. He knows it will lead to discrimination or racism. God loves each and every one of us, no matter what. You should tell the LGBTQ society that too, and instead of shaming them, pray that they have an encounter with God. Not judge them. Learn to have a relationship with God yourself and ask Him what is right; otherwise you're going to be led astray. C'mon Tony, let's go.
Sabrina: (Sarcastically) Whatever you say, pastor Tamika. C'mon Sam.

Samantha then bumped into Mabel before they got to the car.

Mabel: Sammy (getting a hold of her arm).
Samantha: Please don't (releasing her arm from Mabel).

Mabel just stood there with her yellow dress whipping whenever the wind licked it. She didn't know that it was a symbol of how her joy was going to be licked away from her and turned to misery. They got into the car and it was the heated topic on their journey home.

Kevin: Today the pastor spoke.
Sabrina: Right, and can you believe the nerve of Tamika? She says we shouldn't judge them but love them.
Liam: But isn't it the honest truth? The LGBTQ society is a wretched society. Why should we love them for wrong?
Kevin: She's no pastor, so she doesn't know what she's saying. Those people are abnormal.
Sabrina: It's just disgusting.
Liam: Those people should be arrested because that's a crime.
Kevin: You're right son. They should suggest that. It will solve this problem.
Sabrina: True. I never thought of that. That's a smart idea.
Liam: Ey sis, why the silence? Don't tell me you are in support of what your boyfriend's mom said?

During the conversation Samantha had been looking out the window, and tear droplets had been trickling down her face. Samantha didn't turn around to look at her brother as it would have been obvious she was crying, and the question of why she was crying would have popped up, and she would have to come up with an explanation.

Samantha: (Tears trickling down her face) Tony is not my boyfriend. Please don't get me involved in this and may I please have my cap?
Sabrina: What for? You heard what the pastor said.
Samantha: Mom, may I please have my cap!?
Kevin: Don't raise your voice at your mother young lady.
Sabrina: Owwkay. No need to yell...Teenagers!
Liam: Excuse me. Be specific. Samantha!

Samantha was given her cap, and she wore it low so that she could cover her eyes to hide their swollenness and redness. She quickly got out of the car and went straight to her room, where she cried all the pain she was feeling. She also wrote in her diary.

15/10/21

Dear Diary

I've tried everything, and I mean everything, and I don't seem to just fit in. Today we went to church and I was told I'm going to hell if I'm lesbian, which I am. Maybe it's true, but for once in such a long time I had fallen in love with someone who loves me, but I guess I have to let her go. I don't know what to do anymore. I'm stuck inside a world I hate. My happiness is like looking for keys in a couch, so hard to find. I doubt I'll ever be happy cause no one loves me, and no one understands me. Who am I? I used to have an answer to that, but now I really don't know.

S.H.C.

CHAPTER 5

From that day onwards her heart never belonged in her chest. It didn't seem to even exist. She looked at herself in the mirror and banged it. It cracked and she decided to shatter it all completely. While she was doing so, she cut herself on her left arm, and she quickly rushed herself to the bathroom in her room and wrapped it up. She also got some bruises on her face from the way she was violently cracking the mirror. She put the glass in the recycle bin and there was no mirror in her room anymore. She thought it would solve her problems.
She went to school that week and she also took out the mirror in her locker. She cut herself once again, but on the right arm and on her cheek. Luckily, she had a first aid kit in her locker, cleaned herself up and bandaged herself.

She bumped into Mabel that day.

Mabel: Babe, we need to talk. I know Sunday service was one of the most painfu... Sammy, what happened to you?
Samantha: I cut myself with glass.
Mabel: Intentionally or...
Samantha: ...It was an accident. Listen Mabe, you can no longer be my girlfriend. The world is against it.
Mabel: So, you live for the world Sammy?
Samantha: This is the world we live in. I'm sorry...
Mabel: ...Sorry! You're breaking up with me over words. As far as I know, a Christian doesn't judge anyone but loves them, which includes tolerance and respect.

Samantha: You're no pastor, Mabel. We both know that this was wrong and the only way for the church to fix us was to intimidate us.

Mabel: So, fear and not faith is the solution. You're right, it's wrong, but is it like we can't just be friends? Samantha, you're a broken soul, you won't achieve anything by living for other people. You need to live for you. The pastor is a human being. He's not God, so he can't make the decision of whether or not we'll go to heaven or hell. It's between you an...

Samantha: ...I don't want to hear it Mabel. I don't need a lecture. I don't need you, okay? Just stay away from me. It's for the best.

Mabel: But Sam, you don't really mean...

Samantha: (Looking her straight in the eyes) ...I mean it.

Samantha then closed her locker and walked away. She went to the ladies' room and cried like never before. She was truly broken. Everything had just been a dead end. A complete failure. She looked at herself in the mirror and splashed it with water.

Samantha and Mabel grew apart, and it was so short-lived, like a poem just left midway but deserving so much more detail.

One day she bumped into Tony at her locker, who she had been also avoiding.

Tony: Wow, Sam. So I no longer exist anymore? Mabel told me everything. Are you alr... yikes! You look a mess. What goes on?

Samantha: (Putting her hoodie on) Sorry. I've not been in the best of moods.

Tony: I understand. That's why I'm here for you.

Samantha: You don't understand.

Tony: Sam, c'mon, wait, where is your mirror?
Samantha: I shattered it, that's how I got hurt so much.
Tony: But you love mirrors.
Samantha: What's the point when all I see in the mirror is a phantom, Tony, or just... nothing at all.
Tony: Ummm.
Samantha: You know what, forget it.

Samantha just walked away and left Tony there in a state of confusion and uneasiness. Samantha became the definition of gloom. Hopefully it wouldn't lead to doom. There was a time when her mom came into her room, and she was sat by the window staring at the moon.

Sabrina: Okay Sam, where are your dirty clothes?
Samantha: In the washing bucket Mother.
Sabrina: Okay. Mother! Is everything okay Sam?
Samantha: Yes, why wouldn't it be?
Sabrina: I mean sounding weird, looking at the moon and being awfully quiet is a little suspicious.
Samantha: Force of habit.
Sabrina: Owwkay. How come all your clothing is now in black? There is no color whatsoever.
Samantha: I like black and decided to have all my clothing in black. Black is bold, right?
Sabrina: What of the mirror?
Samantha: It was a distraction, so I shattered it.
Sabrina: Owwkay then. I'll just be leaving.
Samantha: Mmhm.

Sabrina left, though she was unsettled. Was this normal? Was this how teens of this generation were?

What she didn't know was Samantha had grown so numb. Numb to emotions. Numb to pain. Numb to her friends. Numb to her family. Numb to people and numb to the world. Even when her results came out and she had 2As, 7Cs and a D, which was in Literature because of Mr Richards. As usual, her parents yelled at her and compared her to Liam, who had 10As and made her feel worthless, like she was not capable of anything. She just kept quiet, didn't argue, didn't complain and didn't say a word until they were all done and blurted out a swift "Sorry, it won't happen again. I promise." She walked away with her report card and left everyone in the lounge speechless.

Promposals were in the air. In class, Randy bumped Samantha when he walked past her and asked Kenzie to be his prom date. After Kenzie said yes, he kissed her and looked at Samantha who just rolled her eyes and looked away. Everyone got a prom date except Samantha, that is until...

Tony: Hey Sam.
Samantha: Hi.
Tony: Here (giving her a red rose).
Samantha: What's this for?
Tony: For you and um, could you come to my locker for a sec?
Samantha: Umm, why?
Tony: There's something I need to show you.
Samantha: Owwkay.
Tony: Open it.

Samantha opened his locker and confetti splashed her, and a promposal pop-up came out.

Samantha: Nawww Tony. Yes, I'll go with you to the prom.
Tony: Really? Great!
Samantha: Are you sure you want to go with me to prom though?
Tony: Absolutely!

Samantha: (With a slight smile) If you say so.

The day arrived and she was like a dark princess from Gotham City. Samantha wore a black gothic dress and black heels, she also asked Tony to get her a black corsage. She also wore black eyeshadow, black lipstick, black nail polish, a black spade necklace, a black nose ring, a black spade ring and some black spade earrings. Tony arrived and waited 10 minutes till...

Sabrina: Samantha! Tony is here.
Samantha: Coming!
Sabrina: I'm sorry Tony. You know girls.
Tony: It's alright, Mrs Carter. It's not a big de...

Samantha walked down the stairs like a gothic highness.

Liam: Uhhhh!
Kevin: What in the world!?
Sabrina: Is this a Gotham-themed prom!?
Tony: (Dreamily) You look bold.
Sabrina: BOLD!? Bold!? That's not bold. That's dark and evil. Samantha, couldn't you get a pretty pink dress?
Samantha: As I said before Mother, I prefer black. Tony did you bring my corsage?
Tony: (Refraining from gazing at Samantha) Uhh, yeah, right here. Here you go (putting a black corsage on her wrist).
Sabrina: It's black.
Samantha: Of course. I'll be back at 9:00pm sharp. Let's go Tony.

Tony and Samantha left for the prom. Samantha was awfully quiet most of the time. Tony asked her to slow dance, and as they did she looked at Kenzie and Randy, who were busy kissing each other. She looked at the other side and saw Katey with Todd. Katey just rolled her eyes and kept slow dancing with Todd. She looked at the serving counter and there was that lunch lady. One of the chaperones was Mr Richards, who glared at her. She turned away and, to her dismay, there sat Mabel. She drank some punch all alone. She locked eyes with Samantha. A teardrop formed a stream down her blossom cheeks, and she brushed it off and looked away. Samantha was shattered. She could feel the pain she had inflicted on Mabel, and tears formed in her eyes too.

Tony: Sammy. Are you okay?
Samantha: Mmm (blinking her tears away). Oh yeah, yeah. It's nothing.

Tony drew her close, hoping it would make her feel a bit better, but then, all of a sudden, she started having flashbacks to all the name-calling. She got so overwhelmed and started breathing heavily.

Samantha: (Trying to breathe normally) I...I need...I need some air.
Tony: Yea sure. C'mon.

Tony and Samantha went outside.

Samantha: I'm sorry Tony. I'm just ruining your prom dance.
Tony: Oh no. Don't worry. Are you alright though?
Samantha: (With a forced smile) Uh, yea. I'm fine.
Tony: So, let's go back in and party.
Samantha: You know what? Actually, I really want to go back home. I'm just not in the mood anymore. I never was to be honest.
Tony: Oh I, um, I see.
Samantha: Tony, it's not you, no, it's just that... (with a sigh) it's complicated.
Tony: I get it. I'll just drop you off.

The entire journey back to Samantha's house, Samantha and Tony did not converse about anything.

Tony: (Opening the door for Samantha) Here you go.
Samantha: Thank you Tony. Listen, about back there. I meant…
Tony: …You don't need to explain. There's a lot on your mind. You need to clear your mind.
Samantha: (Smiling) You understand me so well.
Tony: If you need anything. Anything at all. I'm here.
Samantha: I know, but I'll be fine. Bye Tony (giving him a hug).
Tony: Bye Sam (giving her a hug).

Tony drove home while Samantha went to her room.

Sabrina: You're back already.
Kevin: An hour early.
Liam: Is it like Tony betrayed you?
Samantha: You're all about seeing me as a nuisance Liam. Is that it?
Liam: Well, a nuisance is just one of the terms I use for you. I mean, there is idiot, stupid, dumb, weak, ugly…
Samantha: …Go on Liam. You can't end there. It must be such an uplifting feeling to demean me, especially in my state.
Liam: Uh, well, when you say it like that…
Samantha: …Save it, Liam Brave Carter. I came home early because I felt like it. I'm off to my room now. Goodnight.
Sabrina and Kevin: (In chorus) Goodnight.

Samantha went into her room and looked at herself in the reflection on her window. Her body was so structurally shaped. She felt so insecure about it. She looked away and changed into her pajamas, and again her reflection stared at her. Her head started spinning and she couldn't bear it. She lay on her

bed, and flashbacks came to settle in her mind once again.
Now, all the name-calling, all the bullying, all the harassment, all the degrading, all the comparison, all the injustice. It clouded her. Tears ran down her face, and that entire night she lay twisting and turning, thinking about everything. She wanted a solution. One that would solve everything. One that would fix everything. One that was quick, and she was desperate. She wrote the last pages of her diary and clipped it with a bookmarker. She then sent a message to Tony to bring her something the following day and then went to sleep.

CHAPTER 6

The next morning was the last day of the school term. The last day of the school calendar for that year. Next year would be different. Absolutely different. Samantha wore an oversized black hoodie and some black sweats with a pair of black sneakers.

Sabrina: Alright, everyone! Let's...Samantha?
Samantha: (Avoiding looking at her) Morning Mom.
Sabrina: You're up early. I mean, it's been a hectic year for you, so I can understand why you want it to be over so soon.
Samantha: (Biting her apple) Mmhm.
Sabrina: Owwkay then. Liam!
Liam: Coming! (Running down the stairs) Someone's already here (removing Samantha's hood).
Samantha: (Putting it back on.)
Liam: You're no fun, you know that?
Samantha: (Tightening the strings of her hoodie.)
Kevin: You people are actually early today (giving Sabrina a kiss). I gotta get going. I have a meeting. Are you okay Samantha?
Samantha: I will be okay.
Kevin: Will be or am? Someone has to work on her tenses. I've got to go. Bye.
Sabrina, Liam and Samantha: (In chorus) Bye!
Samantha: I love you Dad.

Kevin: Uh, I love you too Sam.

Mr Carter was perplexed. Samantha had never been so sentimental like that with him before. It shocked Mrs Carter and Liam too. Samantha just finished her apple quietly.

Sabrina: Owwkay then. We better get going.
Liam: Yep.

They drove to school and were dropped off.

Sabrina: Bye you two!
Liam and Samantha: (In chorus) Bye Mom!
Samantha: (Giving her mom a bear hug) I love you with all my heart. (In a whisper) Bye.
Sabrina: (Hugging her back) Umm, I love you too. Bye baby (giving her a kiss on the forehead).

Sabrina just left, but she felt like she had not said a proper goodbye. She felt unsettled and uneasy and, most of all, worried.

Liam: What was that all about?
Samantha: For old times' sake.
Liam: Is everything okay? I know I'm not the touchy, feely type, but I'm curious. You are my little sis. Man, that took guts. Anyway, soo...
Samantha: Everything will be.
Liam: Are you sure?
Samantha: I promise. (Hugging Liam) I love you.
Liam: (Hugging her back) I uhh, I love you too.

Samantha just walked to class, leaving her brother in a state of confusion.

Tony: Hey Sam.

Samantha: Hi Tony.
Tony: Last day of the school year.
Samantha: Tell me about it. It soon will be all over, as if it never existed.
Tony: Yea, uhhh, what? By the way, before I forget, here is the rope you asked for.
Samantha: Thanks Tony.
Tony: Out of pure curiosity, why did you ask me to get that rope for you?
Samantha: Oh that, I have this project.
Tony: Oh. What is it about?
Samantha: You'll see soon enough.
Tony: Okay.
Samantha: Tony, I just wanted to say you're the best, and you mean the world to me. I'm grateful for everything.
Tony: Oh it's no...

Before he could finish his statement, she kissed him.

Samantha: See you in class.
Tony: Uhhh, yeah, class.

Tony could not believe what had just happened. It felt like a dream. For a moment he thought about the rope he had given to Samantha, but then, because of the kiss, he did not think too much about it. He had finally gotten a kiss from Samantha. Perhaps this was it, perhaps he could finally ask her, tell her, confess to her how he felt for her after all these years they had known each other.

Samantha then bumped into Mabel at her locker.

Samantha: (Clearing her throat) Ahem.
Mabel: Samantha? What's up?

Samantha: I just came to apologize for what happened between us. I should have treated you better.
Mabel: Ohh that. It's in the past.
Samantha: So, we're cool?
Mabel: We're cool. So, can we still be friends?
Samantha: Let's make these few moments count.
Mabel: Yea, umm?
Samantha: It's nothing. I'll see you in class. Bye.
Mabel: Bye Sam.

Teachers came in that day to tell them who was taking their classes the following year.

Mr Richards: So, class. I was not supposed to take you next year, but due to circumstances... (looking at Samantha), Eyy Samantha, get rid of that hood.
Samantha: (Removing her hood) Sorry sir.
Mr Richards: You see what I'm talking about. This, this is the behavior I need to straighten out.

Samantha put up her hand.

Mr Richards: What!? What is it Samantha Hope Carter!?
Samantha: May I please be excused?
Mr Richards: Whatever. Just go.

Samantha stood up and went past Tony's desk.

Samantha: Please never forget me.
Tony: Huh?
Mr Richards: Miss Carter, is that the lavatory?
Samantha: Sorry sir.

Samantha took one last glance at the entire class and Tony. She wore her hoodie and took the rope she had asked for from

Tony in a text the previous night and put it in her pocket where she put her hands. She just looked down, and as she was lost in her thoughts, she bumped into Randy.

Randy: Watch it! Oh, it's you.
Samantha: Sorry Randy.
Randy: Yea, yea. Whatever. Where are you going? The ladies' room is in the other direction.
Samantha: I know. I have some unfinished business.
Randy: Like what?
Samantha: That's none of your business.
Randy: Owwkay.
Samantha: Bye forever Randy.
Randy: What?

Samantha then walked away. She went into the woods near their school.
Later on, at break, Tony looked for Samantha.

Tony: Ey Mabel.
Mabel: Tony (removing breadcrumbs from her face). What is it?
Tony: Have you seen Sam?
Mabel: The last I saw of her was in class and just before when she was acting weird. You know, she even said, "Let's make these few moments count." Wasn't that weird?
Tony: Yea that was. Umm, thank you. If you see her, tell her I was looking for her.
Mabel: Sure thing.

He talked to Katey.

Tony: Ey Katey.
Katey: (Acting nervous and playing with her hair) Hi Tony.
Tony: Have you seen Sam?

Katey: (Stops playing with her hair) Wow!
Tony: What?
Katey: Nothing. No, I haven't. Last time I saw that brat was in Mr Richards' class.
Tony: Okay thanks.

He talked to Kenzie

Tony: Hi Kenzie.
Kenzie: Tony. What do you want?
Tony: I'm looking for Sam. Have you run into her, perhaps?
Kenzie: You're asking me. I would not be near as close as a centimeter in her vicinity. If you didn't know, I don't...
Tony: ...don't like her. I know. Thanks.

Tony Talked to Liam.

Tony: Hey Liam.
Liam: What's up Tony?
Tony: Oh, nothing much. Have you seen Sam?
Liam: Uhh no. Last time I saw her was just before school started. Why do you ask?
Tony: I can't seem to find her. She's just gone missing.
Liam: What!? My sister.
Randy: So, she is your sister?
Liam: (To Randy) Shut up squirt. (To Tony) She's always with you. Where could she have gone?
Tony: I really don't know.
Liam: And she was acting so weird today. She hugged Dad, Mom and me and told us she loved us. She even said, "Everything will be okay," when I asked her if everything was okay. We have to find her. If you see her, tell me and I'll tell you if I do too.
Tony: Yea sure.

Tony also talked to Randy.

Tony: Randy.
Randy: (Making a signal to his teammates to tell them to scatter) Tony, hey. Look, I don't want any trouble. I just bumped into your girlfriend by mistake.
Tony: What? Wait, you saw Sam? Where is she? For the record, she's not my girlfriend.
Randy: Oh, I didn't know that. Yea, I saw her after she exited Mr Richards' lesson. She was wearing her hoodie, and she bumped into, I mean, I bumped into her by mistake.
Tony: How was she acting, and where did she go?
Randy: To be honest. Please don't hurt me. She was acting quite funny, and she even said, "I have some unfinished business." I don't know what that even meant but she seemed like she was heading out of school.
Tony: What!? (Holding Randy's collar) And you let her? Now I'm really going to hurt you.
Randy: She said it's none of my business, man. Please don't.
Tony: Argh (letting go of his collar). Maybe she went to get ice cream. If you see her again, please tell her I'm looking for her.
Randy: Absolutely.

Teachers came in after break and still no Samantha. Tony was starting to get worried.

Miss Paris: Here are your forms. Where is Samantha?
Everyone: (Turning to look at Tony.)
Tony: I don't know. If I see her, I'll give them to her.
Miss Paris: Uh huh. Is she okay?
Tony: I think so?
Miss Paris: You **think** so? You don't know so?

The siren wailed and that was the end of the school calendar for that year.

Miss Paris: Alright, everybody. Come take your forms.

Tony made his way out and tried calling Samantha again. This time a message said the number was unreachable, yet all the other times it had been ringing, but there was no answer.

Liam: Have you seen my sister?
Tony: No. I haven't. I've tried calling her, but nothing.
Liam: Let me try. (He tried calling his sister, but the message read: "Unreachable.") That's weird. When you called her, did it do this?
Tony: It was ringing before but now it's saying unreachable.
Liam: You know what? Maybe she went home early. I'll let you know when I get home.
Tony: I'll just linger around here for a while.
Liam: Yea you do that.

Liam took the bus home and got into the house.

Liam: Sam! Samantha! Hope! Sis! Where could she be?

He noticed that she had left her diary on her bed and a note written "READ ME PLEASE!" He opened her diary and read where the bookmark was. He started crying. He called his mom immediately. Meanwhile, his mom was really uneasy about what had happened that morning with Samantha.

Mary: Sabrina dear. You have been in such a downpour mood today. Is everything okay?
Sabrina: Yea, it's just Sam. You know…
Mary: …Oh, tell me about it. These teenagers of ours. So stressful. You know Craig actually…

Sabrina then got a phone call from Liam.

Sabrina: Sweetheart, calm down. What is it?...What!?...No! ... She wouldn't!...She couldn't! (Tears started rolling down her cheeks.)
Mary: Is everything okay Saby?
Sabrina: No! No, it's not. My Sammy! My baby!
Mary: What is it? Calm down Saby!
Sabrina: Oh, shut up Mary! Let me be. I need to go now.

Sabrina ran to her car and went to pick up Liam, who was still crying and reading his sister's diary. Sabrina also called her husband and told him what was going on. He couldn't believe it and drove to the school, where he met up with his emotional wife and son.

Tony: (Speaking to himself) Man, where could that girl be? (With a sigh) Woah, isn't that Samantha's mom and dad's cars?
Principal Penolopy: Tony, is it true what I'm hearing? You're Samantha's best friend right?
Tony: Uh, yeah, what is it?
Sabrina: (Yelling and crying) Where is my baby? I want my baby! Principle Penolopy! Is she really not here!?She better be here and not in the woods!
Principle Penolopy: Mrs Carter, may you please calm down?
Sabrina: (Yelling and crying) Don't tell me to calm down!
Liam: Principle Penolopy, please. You need to help us.
Tony: (Whistling) Ey! Can someone tell me what's going on here?
Principal Penolopy: You seriously don't know?
Kevin: Samantha wrote in her diary that she's going to take her own life today in the woods, and if she did it, then it must have been a few hours ago.

Tony: What!?
Sabrina: Suicide! Why suicide!?
Tony: (In a whisper) She wouldn't.
Sabrina: That's what I thought Tony, but hey. Oh my daughter...

At that moment, Tony's mom arrived.

Tamika: You're in big trouble, young man. Weren't you supposed to come back an hour ago?
Tony: Mom, not now please.
Tamika: Woah, what's going on here?
Sabrina: Samantha committed suicide in the woods!
Tamika: What!? Impossible! She couldn't.
Sabrina: Well she did. She wrote it here in black and white.
Tamika: Wait, you haven't seen her yet. What if she's still alive? Call the police and let's go look for her in the woods. Maybe she couldn't go through with it.
Liam: Tony's mom is right. We have to see if she actually did it because right now we are basing it on black ink and white paper claiming she took her life in the woods.
Kevin: (Trying to comfort his wife) They're right honey. Let's just try.

Police officers arrived, and the scavenger hunt for Samantha began. People shouted, yelled and called out her name, but no response.

Liam: Check it out.
Tony: Explains why she wasn't responding to our calls.
Liam: Right.
It was Samantha's phone. It looked like a snail that had been run over by a car.

Police officer Cathy: She must have crushed it with this rock. Fellas, could you please come check this out? C'mon, we have to find her.

They searched for hours until...

Kevin: I'm about to give up. Maybe she ran away.
Sabrina: Shut up Kevin! She's here somewhere. I just know it.
Tony: No kidding (falling to his knees). There she is (pointing to a tree that was near the calmly flowing Middletown River. There hung Samantha's corpse.)

Sabrina gave out a scream.

Tamika: She actually went through with it (she hugged her son who was crying).
Liam: Of all the things Samantha. Why suicide? (Tears paved their way down his cheeks).
Kevin: (Hugging his wife and a tear droplet drawing its pathway down his cheek.)

This would have been what would resonate powerfully with the song "I Lost a Friend" by FINNEAS.

CHAPTER 7

The police quickly cleared the scene, and the following days were filled with interrogations. This was what was written on the last pages of Samantha's diary...

30/11/21

Dear Diary and anyone who reads this:

I write this as it might be the last thing I write forever. I have been going through so much, and no one seems to understand me. It started at the beginning of this year when I gained a few kilograms and people fat-shamed me. From people like my family to my colleagues, to people like Mr Richards, who humiliated me, to social media. I was so uncomfortable in my own body. This made me think that the solution was to lose the weight. That's what I did, but that just brought out skinny shaming. I was constantly made fun of for losing weight and was made hysterical by people from every direction. I couldn't even celebrate my birthday and have a birthday party because I had the constant pressure to look good. I then decided to work out and get the so-called "perfect body" (with everything in its correct proportions). Little did I know that I was going to be slut shamed and sexualized. I got into so many uncomfortable situations that included assault and even attempted rape by Randy. I tried covering up the curves, but that just made me seem like I was a boy. I then decided to try girls and dated Mabel, but the whole universe was against it. I guess it was not right but the way people blew it out of proportion was just uncalled for. I then had to break up with Mabel, causing a drift in our relationship. Mabel, if you do read this, I once again am really sorry.

You deserved better. You were right, I was so caught up in trying to please everyone that I couldn't please myself. You will find someone but that someone isn't me. You will always be one of my closest friends. As for Mom and Dad. I love you though the way you used to treat me was just heart-breaking. The constant comparing of Liam and me and to my disadvantage as I wasn't as smart as Liam, I wasn't as confident as Liam, I wasn't as liked as Liam, I wasn't as popular as Liam. The fact on ground is I just wasn't Liam and never was going to be. You also never gave me a chance to speak or a platform to say my opinion. It was like I was a nuisance, or it was all in my head, or I was an attention seeker, or I was just...a girl. If only you knew this, maybe things would've been different, and honestly it would have been nice to be treated as two different individuals, with different capabilities but equally with no favoritism or comparison. Liam, my dear brother. Siblings will be siblings. Though I would've really liked it if you didn't look down upon me or degrade me. It might have been because of our parents that you had this mentality, but a true sibling and a true brother would stand by his sibling. You could have stopped the comparing, you could have protected me from the name calling, you could have helped me in my school work, but you didn't. It broke me and made me feel all alone. To Mr Richards. Your crimes are going to catch up to you. It's just a matter of time. I might not see it with my own eyes, but mark my words, what happens in the dark always comes to light. My beloved second mother, Ms Tamika, I know I should've listened to you more. I would not have gone through with this. I should have loved and appreciated myself more for the way I was. I'm sorry Mom but the pressure got to me and it was just so overwhelming. Last and certainly most importantly, Tony. Tony, you are the one I have to apologize to the most. What I did to you was just so unfair. You should've told me how you felt and I wouldn't have this guilt. I recently found out that you loved me, but I had no idea. You were such a great guy ever since we were just in preschool. When I started my grade three at the same school you went to, you made me feel accepted. You have always been there for me, being my number one supporter, protecting me (I especially thank you for what happened at the party. If it wasn't for you, God only knows what would've taken place, for also trying to make me love myself and for being the best friend a girl could ask for).

You deserved to be more than just my best friend, and that's for sure. We should've dated, but to be honest it would have been wrong for you to date me, for it would seem like you were the last option. You were supposed to be the first. FYI, Katey didn't like me because she liked you. It wasn't only because I beat her in our studies and became the best Literature student but because I was closer to you than she was to you. I'm sorry Katey for taking your friend. Tony, you have a big loving heart. Someone will love you, but that someone isn't me. You will always belong in my heart. For everyone, let's not give in to male fantasies and expectations. Girls are not based on what they wear or what they look like. They are based on who they are, their personality. Kenzie, you should also know that. I know you had a grudge with me ever since I beat you and became the best gymnast in grade 3, but giving me a spot on the cheer squad was all I wanted. I didn't want to argue with you, but a place where I could express my talent. Anyway, it is what it is. Don't only teach girls to cover themselves and shy themselves into the dark and, in other words, be afraid of guys, but empower them to become strong and independent. Make them go for self-defense classes, make them join karate and it could make such a difference. As for the boys, teach them to have self-control and not to just see girls as objects they can take advantage of or do whatever they like with, but to see them as subjects of society who deserve respect, love and honor. If we don't teach the young ones, this is going to be prevalent in many generations to come. If you lose yourself, you'll lose it all. I end this by saying how much I truly love you all and how I forgive you and hope you all have blessed lives.

Yours

~~*Samantha Hope Carter*~~

One could feel the brokenness of this young 17-year-old girl. She had really written all that was heavy on her heart, and though she had taken her life, she had put it to the world to be aware of these things and learn from them, because those who don't learn from history repeat it.

The report then finally came out.

Officer Cathy: A moment of silence for the recently departed Samantha Hope Carter.... Right, good morning ladies and gentlemen. I'm here to present the report on Miss Samantha Hope Carter's passing. What happened on the 1st of December is that after she left Mr Richards' "lesson" she left the school premises while the guard was fast asleep. We assume that she left at around noon, and after she left the school premises, she got into the woods. She cracked her phone with a rock so no one could contact her or locate her. She then walked west to the Middletown River, where she hung herself with rope, which she had been given by a friend of hers, Tony Goodness Brown, at around one in the afternoon and laid her soul to rest. Information from the post-mortem diagnoses showed that she was suffering from high levels of anxiety as well as depression disorders that were based on the circumstances she was facing in her daily life. I urge you all, especially the parents, to be aware of mental disorders and not just the physical ones, as we see that we have lost a loved one to suicide because of these very disorders. Mental awareness is real, and let's all treat each other the way the Bible stated in the golden rule: "Do unto others as you would want them to do unto you." As for Mr Richards, he has not only been charged with sexual assault towards the late Samantha Hope Carter, but with various other sexual assaults and sexual harassment in cases of both girls and boys from other schools and neighborhoods. He has also been charged with 3 rape cases, so he is having his court hearing tomorrow. As for the students who were bullying Samantha, they are going to be doing community service for 3 months next year. Tony Goodness Carter...

Some people: Yeah Tony! What about him!?

Officer Cathy: ... He has not been charged with anything, even if he gave her the rope, because he had no knowledge of what she really wanted to do with it, and she even lied to him, telling him that it was for a project. On the other hand, we advise you not to give any of your friends ropes, sharp objects such as razors and knives or any potentially life-taking equipment. Thank you. Have a blessed holiday.

What was painful to know was the fact that even when Samantha was 60kg [132 lbs.], or when she was 50kg [110 lbs.], as well as when she was 55kg [121 lbs.] she was still the right weight for her age. According to her BMI, having a height of 1.60m, she was in the green range for her weight. It was just because she had focused so much on other people's opinions, she did not pay attention to herself.

CHAPTER 8

The holiday was not even a holiday. People did not celebrate it as usual, especially Samantha's family and the Brown family. Tony got so depressed after Samantha's passing that he had to go to therapy. The therapist then noticed that he needed medication and provided him with anti-depressants. The following year he was still just a broken child, and this eventually led to Tony trying to find a way to cure his depression. He ended up abusing different types of drugs to numb his pain, and one day...

Tamika: Tony! Tony Goodness Brown! You are going to be late for school. Tony! (Opening his door) Are you in the bathroom? Tony (knocking on the door). I'm coming in (she screams).

That scream marked another passing. Tony abused drugs, he ended up overdosing on them, and this killed him. Tamika was heartbroken. The report came out just like this:

He had been abusing drugs due to depression, and he actually intentionally killed himself. It must have been because he believed he was the reason for Samantha's death; that, if only he had not given Samantha that rope, it would be a different story. Tamika was so heartbroken and had to go to rehab for major depressive disorder. It was so overwhelming after being physically and emotionally abused by her ex-husband to losing her one and only son, her one and only child, and that was it.

EPILOGUE

This book's primary goal was to spread mental health awareness. Many people tend to dismiss mental health struggles as "all in someone's head," which makes them particularly dangerous. Unlike visible illnesses, mental health issues are often hidden, leaving individuals to suffer alone until their condition becomes severe or even fatal. As a wise woman once said—my beloved biological mother, Lenny Manyemwe—"avoid costs." This means it is far less costly, both emotionally and financially, to support someone who is struggling in the early stages of their illness than to wait until the situation becomes critical and far more challenging to address.

Depression!

Pain is the game,
Like the rain,
My tears pour,
And flow,
Like the thunder,
My headache pounds,
Constant sounds,
Around,
Suppress,
Oppress,
And depress me,
I request,
A quest,
To be joyful,

But I remain sorrowful,
People think all my sighs,
Are just lies,
They think it's not real,
But I've gone through all the bills,
Just like Marylin Monroe,
The lifelong depression was a role,
In taking her soul,
It's all unhappiness,
And sadness,
Grumbling,
And mumbling,
Heartache,
And heartbreak,
This is consuming,
Pauses my life and stops it from resuming,
For God's sake,
It's not fake,
Depression is real,
And a big deal,
Before it's too late,
And conclude it's fate,
Let's assist this emotional,
And psychological state,
Let's not promote sadness,
Unhappiness,
But Mental Awareness.

REFERENCES

Discovery Mood & Anxiety Program | Mental Health Treatment – Depression Symptoms in Teens: Why Today's Teens Are More Depressed Than Ever: https://discoverymood.com/blog/todays-teens-depressed-ever/

Mayo Clinic – Teen Depression: https://www.mayoclinic.org/diseases-conditions/teen-depression/symptoms-causes/syc-20350985

Mayo Clinic – Anxiety Disorders: https://www.mayoclinic.org/diseases-conditions/anxiety/symptoms-causes/syc-20350961

Mayo Clinic – Bipolar Disorder: https://www.mayoclinic.org/diseases-conditions/bipolar-disorder/symptoms-causes/syc-20355955

healthdirect – Bipolar Disorder: https://www.healthdirect.gov.au/bipolar-disorder

Stopbullying.gov – Facts about bullying: https://www.stopbullying.gov/resources/facts

DoSomething.org – 11 Facts about cyberbullying: https://dosomething.org/article/11-facts-about-cyber-bullying

Nemours TeensHealth – Cyberbullying: https://kidshealth.org/en/teens/cyberbullying.html

Johns Hopkins Medicine – Body Dysmorphic Disorder: https://www.hopkinsmedicine.org/health/conditions-and-diseases/body-dysmorphic-disorder

Better Health Channel – Body Dysmorphic Disorder: https://www.betterhealth.vic.gov.au/health/conditionsandtreatments/body-dysmorphic-disorder-bdd

Mental Health Foundation – Millions of teenagers worry about body image and identify social media as a key cause – new survey by the Mental Health Foundation: https://www.mentalhealth.org.uk/about-us/news/millions-teenagers-worry-about-body-image-and-identify-social-media-key-cause-new-survey-mental

OASH | Office on Women's Health – Body Image and Mental Health: https://www.womenshealth.gov/mental-health/body-image-and-mental-health

ABOUT ATMOSPHERE PRESS

Founded in 2015, Atmosphere Press was built on the principles of Honesty, Transparency, Professionalism, Kindness, and Making Your Book Awesome. As an ethical and author-friendly hybrid press, we stay true to that founding mission today.

If you're a reader, enter our giveaway for a free book here:

SCAN TO ENTER
BOOK GIVEAWAY

If you're a writer, submit your manuscript for consideration here:

SCAN TO SUBMIT
MANUSCRIPT

And always feel free to visit Atmosphere Press and our authors online at atmospherepress.com. See you there soon!

ABOUT THE AUTHOR

CHIPO MANYEMWE is an author and poet from Zimbabwe, born on 15 July 2004. She is passionate about fiction. She attended Divaris Makaharis and Monte Cassino Girls' High for primary and secondary education, respectively. Currently pursuing Bachelor's in Computer Applications (Honors) at Parul University in India, she draws inspiration from life itself, music, and past experiences. Known for dialogue-driven stories and vivid characters, she has penned over 70 poems and won a bronze medal on the Allpoetry platform. Chipo aims to craft relatable stories that deeply connect with readers.

www.ingramcontent.com/pod-product-compliance
Lightning Source LLC
LaVergne TN
LVHW092052060526
838201LV00047B/1354